GIB

AND THE

GRAY

GHOST

ZILPHA
KEATLEY
SNYDER

A YEARLING BOOK

35 Years of Exceptional Reading

Yearling Books
Established 1966

Published by
Dell Yearling
an imprint of
Random House Children's Books
a division of Random House, Inc.
1540 Broadway
New York, New York 10036

Visit us on the Web! www.randomhouse.com/kids

Educators and librarians, for a variety of teaching tools, visit us at www.randomhouse.com/teachers

ISBN: 0-440-41518-7

Reprinted by arrangement with Delacorte Press

Printed in the United States of America

November 2001

10   9   8   7   6   5   4   3

OPM

To the memory of three Joes

Chapter 1

As Caesar and Comet trotted down Lovell Avenue, Gib couldn't help turning to look back. Leaning out over the buggy's spinning wheels, he almost forgot to breathe as he watched time and distance shrink the Lovell House Home for Orphaned and Abandoned Boys down to size. All the way down from an evil fairy-tale castle, into a big old ugly mansion house, and finally to nothing more than a dwindling shadow. And then no more Lovell House. Never again, for good and always.

For good and always? Gib took a deep, shaky breath, thinking—well, maybe. Maybe, except for the fact that the whole thing had happened once before.

"What is it, boy?"

It wasn't until she spoke that Gib noticed that Miss Hooper was staring at him. And probably had been the whole

1

time he'd been watching the orphanage fade away to nothing.

"What is it?" she asked again. "Not happy? Not happy to be leaving that dreadful place?"

Gib smiled. "Mighty happy," he said. "And I surely do thank you for . . ." His grin widened. "I surely do thank you and Hy for coming to get me." His eyes moved to where his saddle lay on the seat beside Miss Hooper. "And for saving my saddle too. For talking Miss Offenbacher out of selling it." He shook his head then in a kind of wondering surprise that Miss Hooper had managed to stand up to old Offenbacher and get her to back off.

He was happy. If he'd sighed it had only been because he was remembering how it had all happened before. How he'd left Lovell House that first time heading for a new life with the Thornton family on the Rocking M Ranch. But then it had come to an end, and he'd been sent back to the orphanage. And now the whole thing was happening all over again, just like before. Here he was in the Thorntons' stylish buggy behind the same matched pair of high-stepping bays. The big buggy looked as smart and shiny as it had back then, and Caesar and Comet were as high-stepping as ever, but outside of the team and the buggy there were some important differences.

Of course the biggest change was that when it had happened before, he hadn't known the man who'd come to get him. All he had known was that a man named Henry

Thornton had come to the orphanage looking for a particular boy. A ten-year-old boy named Gibson Whittaker.

But this time Gib knew the people in the buggy well. Both of them. Right there beside him on the driver's seat was good old Hy Carter, who had once been foreman of the Rocking M Ranch, but who was now, at least to hear Hy tell it, nothing more than a bum-legged old handyman. Hy's wrinkle-gullied face and tumbleweed hair looked just about the same as when he and Gib had shared not only his rickety old cabin, but also all the farmyard chores at the Rocking M.

The other buggy passenger was, of course, Miss Agnes Hooper. Thin, sharp-edged Miss Hooper, who had been Mrs. Julia Thornton's friend and companion since she was a little girl—and who was, as of today, Gibson Whittaker's rescuing angel. Gib grinned and when Miss Hooper raised a questioning eyebrow, he said, "I was just thinking as how it was probably the first time anybody ever won an argument with Miss Offenbacher."

Miss Hooper's answering glare didn't scare Gib a whole lot. From long experience he knew that she wasn't nearly as fierce as she looked. Gib's smile widened as he remembered how Miss Hooper's fierce looks used to put him in mind of Bessie, the Thorntons' good-natured old milk cow, who liked to shake her horns at you when you came into the milking shed, seeing if she could spook you some by pretending she was a real dangerous animal.

The buggy was just turning onto Fairfax Street when Gib realized that, in spite of his having two old friends there in the buggy with him, there was a feeling in the pit of his stomach that wasn't entirely comfortable. A feeling that things were changing awfully fast and that he, Gibson Whittaker, had no idea what had caused the change or where it was taking him. It was a scary mixed-up sensation, half hope and the other half dread, and it was a lot like it had been on that other day so many months before. But that time Gib had not even known where he was heading and Mr. Thornton, closemouthed and frowning, surely hadn't been looking to answer any questions.

There had been a lot of questions that Gib had wanted to ask Mr. Thornton back then. And now, on a cold and windy November day in 1909, only a few weeks before Gib's twelfth birthday, there were once again a lot of things he really needed to know. The first question, the one he had to think about for quite a spell before he could make himself come right out and say the words, was about Mr. Thornton himself.

His voice wobbled some when he asked, but Miss Hooper's answer was no-nonsense quick and sharp. "Yes, Gibson, he certainly is. Been dead since the first of last month." She looked at Gib curiously. "But you surely knew, didn't you?" Her ordinary scowl, the one Gib had learned not to take too much to heart, changed into something a lot more serious. A glare that made Gib think of the tight-

4

skinned, flat-eared look of a horse that was about to take a good hard kick at something.

"Do you mean that Offenbacher woman didn't even let you know about Mr. Thornton's death?" Miss Hooper shook her head in a disbelieving way. "Didn't she give you the letter Julia sent you?"

Gib shook his head. "No, ma'am, she didn't tell me. But I knew something had changed, all of a sudden. I heard tell it was maybe 'cause someone had died. And I recollected how Mr. Thornton had been so sickly last spring, so I kind of wondered. But I wasn't sure about—about anything—"

"Changed?" Miss Hooper broke in. "In what way did Mr. Thornton's death change things for you?"

Gib swallowed again and, trying not to make too much of it, he almost managed a smile as he said, "Well, things just got a little bit harder for me a couple of weeks ago. Like a paddling or two, and then my saddle . . ." He paused, struggling to keep the way he felt about his saddle from messing up his voice. "Miss Offenbacher said she was going to sell it." He could tell his voice wasn't cooperating but he went on anyway. "When Mr. Thornton brought me back he got Miss Offenbacher to promise that I could keep the saddle. And she did promise. I heard her promise him, but then all of a sudden she was going to sell it. . . ."

He stopped then, noticing the strange way Miss Hooper was staring at him, and how Hy had turned and was looking too.

5

Miss Hooper muttered something almost under her breath and then went on more loudly. "My fault and Julia's, in a way. She'd been writing the checks and I'd been mailing them, but then when Henry died so suddenly things got neglected for a bit, and . . ." She shrugged angrily. "That evil woman must have decided that, with Mr. Thornton gone, no one would pay them off anymore, or check up on how you were being treated."

Miss Hooper made a fierce snorting noise and turned suddenly to look toward the orphanage as if she was considering going back to tell Miss Offenbacher a thing or two. Gib didn't say anything, but just thinking about a really angry Miss Hooper marching into Offenbacher's office helped him to swallow the lump in his throat and even grin a little.

"And Mrs. Thornton and Livy?" he asked, and then corrected himself. "Olivia, I mean. How's Miss Olivia?"

Miss Hooper huffed a couple more times before she answered, "Well, it's all been very hard on Julia, of course. And on Olivia too." She sighed. "Olivia felt quite close to her father when she was younger, in spite of—" She broke off, paused, and then went on, "But now that the funeral is over and things are getting back to normal, I expect they'll both be doing much better."

Gib nodded and said he surely hoped so, before he went on to the next question. The one that had been bumping against his teeth ever since he got into the buggy. Turning toward Hy, he asked, "And Black Silk? How's Black Silk?"

Hy grinned. "The mare's fine," he said. "Getting purty fat and sassy, though, with nobody on the spread who's up to givin' her a real good workout. I saddled her up once or twice since you . . ." He paused and cleared his throat before he went on, grinning, "since you got the boot, but cain't say I give her much of a ride." He sighed, patted his bad leg, and started going on about all the things he couldn't do a first-rate job of anymore without "really payin' fer it afterwards." He was still describing what a long ride on a live one like Silky did to his "aching old bones" when Miss Hooper interrupted.

"Hyram Carter," she said, "could you forget about your aching bones long enough to ask that lazy team to step it up a little? At this rate we'll all be frozen solid before we get back to the ranch."

Hy grinned at Gib and, as Hy shook the reins ever so slightly, Comet twitched his left ear and Caesar flicked his tail. Gib swallowed a laugh, noticing how the old bays were giving Hy notice that they were at least considering his request. Considering, maybe, but not doing anything much about it. On the buggy's backseat, Miss Hooper went on grumbling and tucking herself into her blankets, and Gib drifted back into silent amazement at the sudden new direction his life had taken, and to wondering what it would all mean in the long run.

Chapter 2

———◆◆◆———

At some point during the long ride from Lovell House to the Rocking M, Gib noticed that his brain was beginning to feel like a mouse in a grain barrel. Like a poor old mouse he'd seen once, spinning one way and then the other without a hope in the world that it'd ever find a way to get out. And it never would have, either, if Gib hadn't given it a little boost with a grain scoop. That had been one confused and scared little rodent, and there were times during that long ride when Gib felt pretty much the same way.

He'd been on some dark and worrisome spins that had to do with Mr. Thornton's death, and with wondering how anybody, especially a person as strong-minded and important as Mr. Henry Thornton, could be right there one day, and then suddenly gone forever. Could be sitting at the head of the dinner table every night reading his newspaper, and driving his new Model T into Longford to the bank each morning, wearing his spiffy gray suits, running the bank and all that was left of the Rocking M Ranch, and then—nothing. No one in his chair at the table, or behind the Model T's steering wheel. No more Mr. Thornton, not ever. Gib had never been able to settle the idea of death into a comfortable place in his mind, and when someone he knew just up and died so suddenly, it seemed especially hard to deal with.

But in between the dark, scary spins, there were some pretty cheerful ones. A lot more cheerful. Like suddenly realizing he might never see Miss Offenbacher again, or Mr. Harding and his paddle. And even better was the spin his mind kept coming back to—the almost certainty that he'd be seeing Black Silk again before the day was over. Over and over again Gib's mind circled around how he'd walk into her stall, watching to see how surprised she'd be, and listening for her welcoming nicker. That was the best spin of all, but there were some others that were almost as good. Ones that had to do with the other horses, and with Mrs. Perry's great cooking, and with seeing Mrs. Thornton again. Mrs. Julia Merrill Thornton, who had been his own mother's friend, and who, according to Miss Hooper, had wanted to really and truly adopt him, way back when he was only six years old and a brand-new orphan.

And then there was Olivia too. Actually he was only guessing that seeing Livy again was something to look forward to. With Olivia Thornton you never knew. He reached into his pocket and brought out the bookmark she'd sent him by way of Miss Hooper. Holding it close to his chest so Hy wouldn't notice, he stared at the picture, sure enough painted by Livy herself. A picture of someone riding a beautiful black horse. The horse was probably meant to be Black Silk, and the rider . . . ? Gib chuckled silently. Livy wasn't much of an artist and the person in the picture could have been almost anybody. Except that the mysterious rider did have long yellow-brown curls and long eyelashes. Gib couldn't help wondering what the picture meant, because nearly everything Livy Thornton did turned out to mean something. But even after a body had figured out the meaning, there were usually a lot of leftover questions that didn't get answered. Actually, thinking about seeing Livy again was one of the things that made Gib sympathize with that trapped mouse. With any poor critter who found himself running around in circles without knowing why he was doing it.

And there were other confusing turns his mind kept taking. As when he asked himself what it would be like going back to live at the Rocking M, now that Mr. Thornton was gone. Would he still be living in Hy's old bunkhouse and working as an orphan farm-out? Or would things be different now without Mr. Thornton, who'd refused to adopt Gib way back when his mother died, and who wouldn't even have taken him on as a farm-out, if poor old Hy hadn't needed help because of his broken leg.

Two or three times as the long flat miles spun past, Gib got himself almost ready to ask Hy or Miss Hooper a few questions, but he never could find words that wouldn't seem pretty cheeky. Words like "Am I still going to be a farm-out, or am I going to be really adopted this time?" Just thinking about asking such an audacious question made Gib's face heat up, and probably turn red too, in spite of the cold prairie wind.

But at last, just as the river was coming into view, he came up with a question that didn't seem quite so cheeky. Turning toward Hy, he said, "Guess I'll be staying in your cabin, like before?"

"What's that?" Hy asked, and when Gib repeated what he'd said, Hy laughed his honking laugh before he turned to Miss Hooper. "Hear that?" he said. "Wants to know if he'll be sleepin' in the bunkhouse tonight. Thought you said he'd been told about the bunkhouse."

Miss Hooper's ferocious scowl was back again. "Are you telling me you never got *that* letter either?" she snapped. "I declare, that Offenbacher woman ought to be arrested for interfering with the U.S. mails."

"You sent me a letter about Hy's cabin?" Gib asked.

"Yes, in part," Miss Hooper said. "About a number of things, actually. But I distinctly remember mentioning in one of my letters that the cabin's roof had pretty much disappeared during that high wind we had last summer. Hy's been living upstairs in the big house since then, and you

11

will be too. Perry and I have a room all made up for you." The pretend frown was back again as she said, "Nothing fancy, mind you, so don't be expecting too much, but at least it will be all yours."

All yours. That was another thought that had Gib's mind spinning during the last few miles before the turnoff. As Caesar and Comet picked up the pace without even being asked to, now that they were close to home, Gib turned over the thought of having a whole room all to himself. How would it feel to go in a room all by yourself and close the door and know that no one else was going to open it unless you told them they could? Gib was still exploring the idea when right there above the road was the wooden sign showing the Rocking M brand. And a couple of minutes later the tall shade trees, the shingled roof, and then the wide porches of the ranch house came into view.

While Hy was still pulling the team to a stop in front of the veranda, Gib jumped down to help Miss Hooper. First of all she had to unwrap herself very carefully from all her robes and blankets. When that was done she started to climb very slowly down the buggy's steep steps, stopping now and then to mutter something under her breath about the long, cold ride and her aching back. By the time she finally was on the ground, the team was stomping and fretting, eager to get to the barn, and Gib was feeling pretty much the same way. Eager to get to the barn, and to Black Silk. He was hurrying as he folded Miss Hooper's lap robes, tucked them over her arm, and handed down her pocketbook. But when he started to climb back up beside Hy, Miss Hooper grabbed him by the back of his coat.

"Where do you think you're going, Gibson Whittaker?" she asked. When Gib said he was going to help Hy put the team away, she went on, "Oh, no, you're not. Not until you come in and say hello. Come in and see the family first. Human beings come before horses, boy, at least for civilized people."

"That's right," Hy said. "You run along and see the ladies. I been taking care of these fat rascals all by myself ever since you got sent . . ." He paused, grinned, and then changed to, "Ever since you left us. One more night ain't going to kill me."

Gib felt embarrassed. He knew Miss Hooper was right, but as he followed her down the path and up the stone steps he told himself that it wasn't just seeing Black Silk that had been on his mind. He'd been thinking about poor old stove-up Hy too, and how he really could use some help with the team. That's what he told himself, anyway, but he didn't tell Miss Hooper because he was pretty sure she'd say it was a good story but she didn't believe it. Gib couldn't help smiling a little as he admitted, to himself at least, that he didn't quite believe it either.

Chapter 3

There it was again, the old ranch house, looking just as solid and everlasting as it had the first time he'd seen it. As Gib went up the broad front steps he put out his hand to touch one of the fat stone pillars that held up the veranda roof, letting his fingertips remember the rough, long-lasting feel of it. A few more steps and there in front of him was the familiar door with its panels of stained glass.

"Well, don't stand there staring, boy," Miss Hooper was saying. "Open the door for me, like a proper gentleman."

Gib jumped to do as he was told, but once inside the wide entry hall he froze again, caught up in a whirlpool of memories. Recollections not so much of the house itself, but of things that had happened there. Things like studying in the library with Miss Hooper as teacher, and with Olivia Thornton as fellow student. And the day he'd stood all alone at the library window just watching while the rest of them went out to admire the family's new Model T. Lost in the memories, he stumbled after Miss Hooper as she stopped, once to peer into the parlor, and then again to hang up her wraps on the hall coatrack.

"Gibson," she said impatiently, "your coat. You can hang it here." Watching him closely as he struggled with the stiff buttonholes in the new mackinaw, she went on, "Hurry along, boy. You seem to be all thumbs today. They're probably waiting for us in the library."

It was then, as the library door opened and the sound of familiar voices drifted out, that Gib realized that his heart was pounding and that something swollen and heavy seemed to be stuck at the bottom of his throat. His feet had gone clumsy and awkward too, so that he stumbled a little as Miss Hooper shoved him ahead of her into the room.

There they all were, looking the same, and yet strangely different. It took a moment for him to realize that part of the alarming difference was only the color black. Black for mourning. Mrs. Thornton, in a high-necked black dress, looked a little paler perhaps, but as elegant as ever. Actually it was Livy, sitting on the sofa with a book in her lap, who seemed to have changed the most. As if a plain black dress instead of ruffled and pleated pinks and greens had suddenly changed a rambunctious eleven-year-old into a proper young lady.

The color black seemed to be everywhere. Even Mrs. Perry, whose dress and apron were flowery gingham, had a black mourning band on her right arm.

They were all looking at Gib. Staring as if they'd never seen him before, or anything like him. Waiting, no doubt, for him to do or say some expected thing. Gib gulped, tried to swallow, and wondered frantically if there was some special way one was supposed to behave around ladies in mourning. Or perhaps something one was supposed to say. The way one said "congratulations" or "many happy returns" for other kinds of special occasions.

Gib was still gulping when Miss Hooper said, "Well, here he is. Rescued by yours truly from the clutches of the Wicked Witch of the West."

Everyone else laughed, and even Gib managed to smile a little, and for a moment, that helped. Gib was just about ready to say hello and how sorry he was about Mr. Thornton's passing on, when Mrs. Thornton held out her hands.

"Gib, dear," she said as she pulled him down beside her wheelchair and gave him a quick hug. "How wonderful to see you again."

It was the hug that did it. Gib's eyes went hot and wet and the lump was back in his throat so big that he nearly choked on it. He stared down at the carpet, feeling tongue-tied and witless, and when he did manage to look up, the amused expression on Livy's face didn't help at all. But then, once again, Miss Hooper came to his rescue.

Taking over, just as firmly as she'd done in Miss Offenbacher's office, she pushed Gib toward a chair. "Sit here, Gibson," she said. "For just a minute." Then she turned to the others. "Gib and I will have to go freshen up soon, but it looks like Delia has something good and warm on that tray, and that's exactly what we need. Came close to perishing of the cold in that buggy. Didn't we, Gib?"

As Gib sat down Mrs. Thornton was saying, "Olivia, dear, could you clear away some of your books so Mrs. Perry can put the tea tray on the table? And Delia. Please sit down and have a cup of tea with us while we all get reacquainted with Gibson."

Then there was the choice of tea or coffee, and cream and sugar, to talk about, and the unusually cold weather for the beginning of November, and how long the trip from Harristown had taken, and after a few gulps of coffee Gib's throat began to relax enough to at least say things like "Yes, ma'am, the wind was right out of the north. Hy thinks it might be fixing to blow up a blizzard," and "No, ma'am, I didn't know Miss Hooper was coming to get me. Not till she showed up."

After that it got easier, because with four talkative ladies in the room, Gib didn't have to say very much. And also because it soon became obvious that it already had been decided that it was too soon to talk about anything important. Anything like why Gib was back at the Rocking M, and what might be going to happen next.

17

And then it was over. Mrs. Perry went back to the kitchen, and Livy went over to crouch beside her mother's chair and whisper in her ear. To whisper and nod, and whisper again, while she watched Gib out of the corners of her eyes. Talking about him, Gib felt sure, or at least pretending to. But then Miss Hooper was ushering him out into the hallway and up the front stairs.

The upstairs in the big house was brand-new territory for Gib. He'd been well acquainted with the kitchen and library, and once or twice Livy had let him peek into the dining room and parlor. But he'd never been down the long hall that led to the new wing of the house, where the Thorntons lived, or up the stairs to the second floor.

At the top of the wide front staircase Miss Hooper led the way down a hallway decorated with striped wallpaper and framed photographs. Lots of old-fashioned pictures of carefully posed families, and then one of a slightly familiar-looking man on horseback. The man was wearing a wide grin and fringed chaps. And the horse, which in the photograph looked to be a light sorrel with a flax mane and tail, was something really special.

Miss Hooper noticed Gib staring at the picture. "That's Daniel Merrill," she said. "Mrs. Thornton's father." Gib wasn't surprised. Something about the shape of the man's face and the high arch of his eyebrows made him think of Mrs. Thornton. Still looking at the photo, Miss Hooper nodded approvingly. "Good man, Daniel was. Built the Rocking M up from a couple of homestead holdings into one of the biggest ranches in the state."

Gib hung back, wanting to ask questions. Questions about Daniel Merrill, and maybe about the sorrel too. But Miss Hooper hurried him down the hall. She pointed out the upstairs parlor and opened the door so he could peek inside. It was a grand-looking room with lots of windows, elegant furniture, and beautiful flowery paper decorating the walls. Gib had never seen anything like it.

"I know," Miss Hooper said in answer to his appreciative gasp. "Very nice, isn't it? Used to be the Thorntons' room until Julia's accident."

"The accident? On Black Silk?"

"Yes, of course," Miss Hooper said. "That's when the new wing was built, because of the wheelchair."

They went on then past the door to Mrs. Perry's room, and past the room which, ever since the windstorm, had been Hy's.

There was a bathroom too, with a claw-foot tub and a washbasin. And next door, in a closet-sized room, a flush toilet. Miss Hooper demonstrated by pulling the chain. "You know how to use this?" she asked Gib.

Gib felt his face getting hot. Looking down at his feet, he mumbled, "Yes, ma'am. I know, ma'am."

"Well, that's good. Didn't mean to embarrass you." Miss

Hooper sounded amused. "But I wasn't sure, since the bunkhouse was a bit short on indoor plumbing, and I can only imagine what the facilities were like at Lovell House."

As they went on down the hall Gib bit his lip, thinking how much he hated it when his face got red like that. When it "flushed" like that, he thought and then grinned, thinking how this time his face had, sure enough, been flushed.

But then Miss Hooper was opening a door at the end of the hall and he forgot about flushing faces and toilets too. Set back under the eaves, the room was smallish, all right, with a slanty ceiling and just one little window. But there were a closet and a chest of drawers, and best of all, instead of a metal cot, a real bed with headboards and footboards made of wood. Real wood, as dark and shiny as a bay horse. Standing in the middle of the room and turning in a slow circle, Gib didn't realize he was smiling until Miss Hooper said, "Well, as I told you, it's not grand, but you seem to be pleased."

"Oh yes, I'm pleased. Mighty pleased, ma'am," Gib said. Before Miss Hooper left she pointed out the alarm clock on the chest of drawers, and the cord that turned on the electric light, and reminded him that dinner was at five-thirty. Her voice was sharp as she said, "Don't you be late, now. And remember to turn out the light when you leave the room." Her thin lips flicked upward in what, for just a moment, came close to being an honest-to-goodness smile before the phony frown returned. Nodding sternly, she said, "Good to have you back, Gibson. Very good indeed."

Gib grinned and said, "It's good to be back." And then, imitating Miss Hooper's frown, he added, "Very good indeed." Miss Hooper went on frowning but her twisted lip and raised eyebrow said she got the joke.

Gib waited only until Miss Hooper's footsteps faded and the door of her room squeaked open and clicked shut before he took a last quick look around and left the room. Almost running now, but very quietly, he went down the hall and the back stairs and out toward the barn. Toward the barn and Black Silk.

Chapter 4

————◆◆◆————

Inside the barn the light was dim, but the air was full of scent and sound. The warm, spicy odor of horse, and the contented rustle and munch of feeding time. Gib breathed deeply and then hurried on, past Comet and Caesar, stopping only long enough to notice that Hy had rubbed them down, at least a little. Busy with their hay, they only flicked an ear when he called their names, before they went back to eating.

Next came Hy's old cow pony, Blue Lightning. The old blue roan was busy eating too but when Gib spoke to him he raised his head, took a step or two toward the stall door, and then snorted softly and went back to his supper. Gib grinned. "Okay for you, you old rascal. Didn't miss you that much either."

The next stall was Black Silk's. By the time Gib reached it she was already at the door. Even in the fading light he could see that she really was as beautiful as he remembered. High crested, short backed, and long-legged, put together just right for speed, and purely black except for the three white feet and the diamond blaze on her forehead. Nodding and nickering, she reached out eagerly toward Gib, her eyes white-rimmed with excitement. Gib opened the stall door, slipped inside, threw his arms around the mare's neck, and buried his face in her long mane.

He stayed there for a quite a spell, while Silky shoved his shoulder with her velvety nose and nickered questioningly. When he was sure he had control of his voice, he began to talk to her, telling her how glad he was to see her again, and how purely gorgeous she was. The most beautiful horse in the whole world, he told her, but then, standing back a way to get a better look, "But not the best groomed, and that's for sure. Looks like you could use a good currying." Silky nodded and nickered as if she understood, and Gib chuckled, remembering how much she'd always liked that old currycomb scratching the itchy places on her withers and back. He checked her feet to see if they were in good shape, and he was just telling her that her hooves surely could use a good picking too, when somebody giggled.

Gib could tell that Olivia Thornton really hadn't grown that much in the three months he'd been away, judging by how much of her face he could see over the stall door. "Hey, Livy," he said.

"Hey yourself," Livy answered. Then she giggled again and asked, "Well, what did she say?"

For a second Gib really didn't know what she was talking about. "What did who say?"

"Silky." Livy sounded impatient. "I heard you talking to her. So I imagine she must have been answering?"

Gib grinned. "Course she did. Said she was right glad to see me again. Said nobody's been taking care of her since I've been away."

Livy frowned. "Well, she's lying then. Hy's been grooming her. And I helped. At least I did right at first. But then, after my father got so sick . . ." She shrugged and looked away.

"Hey," Gib said, feeling mortified that he'd made Livy remember about her dead father. "I was just teasing. She's looking great." He opened the stall door. " 'Cept for her feet. I was just heading down to the tack room to get the hoof pick. Thought I might—"

"You better forget it," Livy said. "At least for now. It's almost suppertime. That's why I came out here. I knew you'd forget about eating once you saw Black Silk." She opened the locket watch that hung around her neck on a gold chain. Turning the watch face toward Gib, she said, "See, already a quarter past."

"A quarter past?" Gib really was surprised. He'd barely have time to get washed up. He turned back long enough to give Silky a good-bye pat and tell her, under his breath, that he'd see her first thing in the morning, before he followed Livy out of the barn.

Livy kept looking at him as they walked across the yard, but if he looked back she tossed her head and turned away. Gib had to squelch a smile, thinking how, in spite of all the changes, some things were pretty much the same. It wasn't until they were going up the back steps that Livy said, "Wait a minute. Before you go in I want to tell you something."

"Okay." Gib stopped on the bottom stair. "Tell me. I'm listening." He pretended to be opening a locket watch and staring at it. "But you'd better keep it short. Looks to be just about suppertime."

She frowned fiercely. "You stop teasing, Gib Whittaker. This is serious." She took a deep breath. "I wanted to tell you . . . I just wanted to say I'm . . . I mean, I hope you don't blame me for getting you sent back to that awful place."

Gib was pretty surprised. Shaking his head in amazement, he said, "I don't blame you. Never did. You didn't know your father was going to come home early and catch you riding Black Silk. Or that he was going to blame me for putting you up to it."

"I know. But it wasn't your fault. You told me not to try to ride her unless you were there, and I said I wouldn't. But then you and Hy were so busy for so long and I just got too impatient and . . ."

"I know." Gib shook his head slowly, remembering how Mr. Thornton had come home in the middle of the day and how Livy, excited and maybe showing off a little, had let the mare get out of hand. "But it wasn't your fault either." He thought a minute and added, "Or Silky's. She didn't mean any harm. But I can see how your father would be real worried because of what happened to your . . ." Noticing the look on Livy's face, he let his voice trail off.

"All right, say it. Because of what happened to my mother." Livy's voice was quick and sharp. "But what were you going to say about my father?"

Gib could see he'd better rein in a little. "Wasn't his fault either," he said quickly. "It must have really scared him the way Silky was acting up. And for good reason too. If you'd been throwed on that hard-packed ground out there, there's no telling what might have happened to you."

Livy shrugged. "You don't have to stand up for him. Nobody does anymore. Not even me." Stomping past Gib, she went on up the stairs and into the house.

By the time Gib had finished at the washing-up trough, Livy was already in the kitchen, helping Mrs. Perry put things on the table. She didn't look at Gib when he came in. And another thing she didn't do was speak to him, not once during the whole meal.

At the table that night Gib learned that no one called Livy's mother Mrs. Thornton anymore. Miss Hooper usually called her just plain Julia, and Mrs. Perry called her Mrs. Julia. Hy had taken to calling her Mrs. Julia too, except he made it sound more like Missus Julia. Gib wondered if all widowed ladies got their names changed like that or if it had something to do with what Livy meant when she said nobody stood up for her father anymore. But whatever the reason, Gib liked the sound of Missus Julia right well, just the way Hy said it.

That night after Gib had used the flush toilet, and flushed it twice just for practice, he had a bath in the claw-foot tub. Lying there in the big shiny white tub in lots of warm water, he thought, first of all, about things like flush toilets and electric lights. He hadn't been lying when he told Miss Hooper that he knew about things like that. Not that there'd been such things at Lovell House. At least not for the orphans to use. But he'd seen lots of electric lights and used a flush toilet too, back in the days when Mrs. Hansen was still alive and the best readers sometimes got to visit the Harristown Library.

It wasn't until his bath was over and he was in bed in his own room that he let himself think about more serious matters.

He thought first off about Jacob and Bobby and his other friends at Lovell House, wishing there'd been time to tell them good-bye, and wondering if he'd ever see them, or even hear from them again. Not likely, he told himself sadly. Not with Miss Offenbacher reading all the Lovell House mail and throwing most of it out. Losing Jacob and Bobby was a sorrowful thought, but at the moment there was another question that was even more troubling.

Lying there in the November chill, tucked in warm and cozy under plenty of quilts and blankets, Gib realized that the most troubling question was what Gibson Whittaker was now. Was he, for instance, still just an orphan farm-out to the Thornton family? Or was he really going to be a part of the family? Or maybe something kind of in between?

Thinking about being adopted made him smile ruefully, thinking of how, now and then, he'd seen a lucky little orphan being toted off to be a real part of a family. Real *little* orphans, they were for the most part. Usually still infants, or no more than toddlers. He couldn't help grinning a little when he pictured Gib Whittaker, a long-legged almost-twelve-year-old, being toted out wrapped in a new blue blanket.

But he stopped grinning then, thinking how most likely he was back at the Rocking M to be exactly what he'd been before: a farm-out orphan whose job it was to help poor old bum-legged Hy take care of chores around the barnyard. Exactly like it had been before, except that he was now living in the big house instead of Hy's tumbledown old cabin.

But Hy was living in the big house now too, and had been since the roof blew off the bunkhouse. And Hy was definitely hired help, so that didn't really prove anything. In fact the whole upstairs was a lot like a bunkhouse now. A bunkhouse where nothing but hired help lived. Hy and Mrs. Perry and now Gib Whittaker, orphan farm-out.

Then again, there had been the feeling tonight that it was sort of a special occasion. Like the supper Mrs. Perry had ready for them. It was in the kitchen as usual, instead of in the grand dining room, but the table had been set with dining room china, and there had been all kinds of great food, including peach pie, Gib's favorite dessert. It didn't seem likely, Gib told himself, that they'd go to that much trouble for a farm-out.

Supper had been different in other ways too. For one thing, there was a lot more talking, and a lot of it had been done by Hy. Gib remembered how one of the things Hy had told him on his very first night at the Rocking M was that the hired help were expected to be *quiet* at the dinner table. Being *quiet* obviously was a rule that nobody cared about anymore. But that difference, Gib decided, probably had a lot more to do with Mr. Thornton's absence than with Gib Whittaker's presence.

When he came to think about it, however, there was another small sign that tonight had been a special event, and that was Livy's locket watch. It seemed to Gib, if he was remembering correctly, that she never used to wear it for just an ordinary day. For churchgoing on Sundays maybe, or if company was coming, but never on a day when nothing important was going to happen.

Gib was still arguing with himself, stacking up all the good signs against the bad ones, when his thinking began to blur some, and the next thing he knew, it was morning.

Chapter 5

When the alarm clock went off its jangling clatter scared Gib half to death. Sitting straight up in bed, he stared around him expecting to see—he didn't know what. A row of metal cots full of sleepy orphans, most likely. While he was still fumbling at the clock wondering how in tarnation you shut the durn thing off, he couldn't help chuckling a little at how he'd bounced himself straight up, as wide-eyed and jumpy as a spooked horse. He found the shut-off switch then and flopped back down under the covers for a minute. Just long enough to get his hackles down and his wits together.

So—it hadn't been a dream after all. Not a hope dream like the ones he'd had as a little kid when, halfway between waking and sleeping, he used to imagine the family he'd someday belong to. And certainly not one of the crazy scenes your mind trots out when you're too sound asleep to care about making sense. Nope. This room was as real and solid as a rock. There he was in a fancy wooden bed under a slanty roof and surrounded by walls covered in flowery paper. It had to be the truth. He really was back at the Rocking M. Glancing at the clock, he saw that it was five-thirty. Just about the time he and Hy had always started the milking and feeding.

Sliding out into the cold air from under the heavy warmth of the blankets, he struggled quickly into his clothing. He tiptoed down the stairs, picked up his mackinaw, and was out the door before he had time to think about what the five-thirty alarm meant. What it meant was—nothing had changed. Just like before, Gib Whittaker, orphan farm-out, was expected to be out of bed and out doing morning chores an hour and a half before breakfast was put on the table.

Hy was already in the barn. "Well, howdy there, pardner," he said as Gib came in. "I been waiting fer you. Right glad to have you back on the job." He didn't have to say that Gib should climb the ladder into the hayloft and throw down the hay while he took care of the water buckets and the oat pails. That was the way it had always been.

Back in Silky's stall after the feeding was finished, Gib barely had time to tell her hello and get started with the currycomb before Hy said, "Awright buckaroo, come along now. Grooming can come later. We got to get them chickens fed and the milkin' done faster'n lightnin' or we'll miss out on breakfast."

But when Gib left off combing, Silky nudged him away from the stall door. "Look," he said, "she doesn't want me to go."

Hy chuckled. "Well, you can just tell that fancy blue-blooded lady that you'll be back later to spruce her up a little. After us two-legged critters git our turn at the feedin' trough."

So everything was back the way it had always been, with the feeding and milking first, and then breakfast. Cleaning up on the back porch, Gib had only a little time to consider what being "back on the job" meant, before he was once again in the good-smelling warmth of Mrs. Perry's kitchen.

As Gib had noticed the night before, the kitchen was a lot noisier than it used to be. Mrs. Perry was scolding Hy for snitching a piece of bacon right off the grill, and Miss Hooper was looking out the window and announcing to anyone in earshot that, for once, Hy's aching bones had been right about the weather. There definitely was a storm blowing up. Missus Julia and Livy, who were already at the table, were busy talking to each other. When Gib walked in everybody stopped long enough to say hello, before they went back to what they'd been doing and saying.

But now Gib talked too. As he ate eggs and bacon and pancakes instead of lumpy oatmeal for the first time in almost four months, he also found himself answering questions. And to his surprise Livy did a lot of the asking. Questions like "How come that headmistress woman let you stay at Lovell House when my father took you back? I thought you said she never let anybody come back once they'd been adopted or farmed out. How come you were different?"

"I don't rightly know," Gib said. "Miss Offenbacher always said no one could come back. I didn't think she'd let me back in either. But when Mr. Thornton . . ." He paused, wondering how to go on. But then Miss Hooper took over.

As Gib smiled inwardly, thinking about all the times she'd come to his rescue lately, she said, "The difference was money. Mr. Thornton offered that Offenbacher woman a good-sized monthly payment if she'd let Gib back into the orphanage. It's as simple as that."

The mention of Mr. Thornton, particularly in the tone of voice Miss Hooper was using, made Gib uneasy. But neither Missus Julia nor Livy seemed upset, so he guessed that it was all right, even though it had sounded pretty much like speaking ill of the dead. However, he was considerably relieved when Missus Julia changed the subject by asking about Black Silk.

"What did she do when she saw you, Gib?" she asked. "Do you think she remembered you?"

Gib nodded hard, swallowed a mouthful of pancake, and

said, "Oh yes, ma'am, she did for sure. She even left off eating her hay to come over to see me. And she made that little whispery nicker like she always does when she's happy about something."

After that the conversation was about horses for quite a spell, with Livy doing a lot of the talking. Livy had a lot to say about how nobody would let her drive the team. Seemed she was pretty unhappy about not being able to go to Longford School anymore because Hy didn't think she could handle a high-spirited team like Comet and Caesar all by herself. But then Hy broke in to say, "No, siree, that warn't it at all, Miss Livy, and you know it warn't. I don't 'spect you'd have any trouble with them old bays. All I said was a little gal like you got no business driving any team out across open prairie all by her lonesome."

But then Missus Julia said, "But that's not going to be a problem anymore now that Gib's here. He'll undoubtedly be going to Longford too, and I'm sure he'll have no trouble with Comet and Caesar."

Gib stared at Missus Julia, wondering if she meant he'd be attending the Longford School too. That seemed like her meaning, but before he could ask to be sure Livy said, "Oh, good. Gib will drive. And he can drive the Model T too."

Gib had almost forgotten about the Model T, which, it seemed, had been sitting uselessly in its garage ever since Mr. Thornton's death. Livy sounded excited as she went on, "Gib could learn how to drive the Model T, and then he can be my chauffeur. How'd you like to be a chauffeur, Gibson?"

Everybody laughed and Gib was saying that he thought he knew a lot more about driving horses than motorcars when Miss Hooper interrupted. "Look at that," she said, pointing to the window. "What did I tell you? It's started already."

They all looked to where a sleety mixture of snow and ice was sweeping across the kitchen window. "Well, that settles it," Miss Hooper said. "Looks like nobody's going to be driving to Longford by any means whatsoever. At least not anytime soon." She sighed. "Which probably means that yours truly is going to be playing the role of reluctant schoolmarm for quite a while longer."

So the blizzard had arrived. Not as bitterly cold as a midwinter blizzard perhaps, but as Hy said, just as wild and woolly, with howling wind and heavy snowfall, and plenty of bone-aching chill. Which meant no Longford School for either Livy or Gib, and no chance to saddle Silky up and ride her out across the prairie. No riding, but plenty of time for grooming and stall cleaning, not only for Silky but the other horses as well.

And, starting on Monday morning, a few hours for Gib and Livy in the library in what Miss Hooper called the Rocking M Institution of Higher Learning. And a lot more time than Gib needed for considering whether he was still only an orphan farm-out, or maybe something more.

Not that he'd really asked. He certainly hadn't asked Missus Julia, who'd never treated him like an orphan nobody, but who wasn't the kind of person you could just up and talk to about personal things. Particularly not now, when she was a new widow, looking pale and delicate in her lacy black dresses.

Gib had always been tempted to stare at Missus Julia, ever since the first time he'd seen her being wheeled into the kitchen in her high-backed chair. He didn't know why for sure. For a time it had been knowing that Silky was hers, and that she'd once been one of the best horsewomen in the whole state. And then, later on, there had been finding out that Julia Thornton had known his own mother, Maggie Whittaker. But, perhaps most important, was when he'd learned from Miss Hooper that Julia Thornton would have adopted Gib right after his mother died, except that Mr. Thornton wouldn't let her.

So there had always been all sorts of audacious questions he would have liked to ask Missus Julia, but for some reason he just couldn't. Not even when they had long talks about other things, like about the old days when her father, Dan Merrill, was alive and the Rocking M was the biggest ranch in the state. Gib particularly liked hearing Missus Julia talk about all the horses she'd owned, clear back to a pinto pony named Dandy her father gave her for her fourth birthday.

Gib liked hearing about Missus Julia's horses. And he especially liked the way her face changed when she talked about them. It seemed to Gib that her face had a healthier color to it and her cough got better too when she talked about Dandy or Silky or any of the other horses she'd owned. Missus Julia was easy as anything to talk horses with, but bringing up things like adoption papers was something else again.

It was with Hy that Gib finally managed to edge up on the adoption question. It was on the second day of the blizzard when the two of them were out in the barn, feeding the stock. Asking Hy any kind of personal question had its good side and its bad side. The good side was how easy Gib felt about asking. The bad side was that, unless the question had to do with horses, Hy probably wouldn't know the answer. Gib decided to ask anyway, but the only answer he got was, "Well now, Gibby. Seems to me as how you're askin' if you're still just a hired hand like old Hy Carter, or if there's going to be some paperwork done that says you're a part of the Thornton family. That it?"

"No," Gib said, "not exactly. Well, sort of . . ."

And Hy chuckled and said he didn't see why it mattered. "Not now anyways. Not now we got ourselves a real Merrill back in charge of the spread agin. Don't matter none that her name's still Thornton, Missus Julia's a real prairie-bred

38

Merrill and always will be. And you can bet your bottom dollar that she'll treat everybody fair and square, jist like her daddy afore her. So don't you go worryin' none about what's put on a piece of paper." Hy hobbled off then, leaving Gib as much in the dark as ever.

Miss Hooper wasn't talking either. Not even when Gib came right out and asked her what kind of paper it was that she'd signed for him that day in Miss Offenbacher's office. Miss Hooper had let school out early that day, because she had a headache and Livy had already disappeared, so Gib thought it was a good time to ask. But when he did, Miss Hooper said that the only signing she'd done that day was on a check.

But if no one else would tell Gib exactly what kind of space he was filling, Livy didn't mind sharing her opinions on the subject. Particularly when she got her dander up over something Gib had done or said. Whenever that happened she could think of things to say that made it pretty clear that, as far as she was concerned, Gib Whittaker was still just an ordinary old farm-out orphan.

Like the time, during an American history class, when Miss Hooper had gone out to get some tea and Livy asked Gib how he'd answered the "Give me liberty or give me death" question. Gib was pretty sure it had been Patrick Henry who'd said it, but when he said so Livy said that she distinctly remembered seeing a picture of Paul Revere shouting something about death and liberty along with the news about the British coming. So she wrote down Paul Revere and when it turned out that Gib was right, she only shrugged a little and pretended she didn't care. But a little later she found a way to get even.

That happened when Miss Hooper asked Gib to explain the difference between renting and leasing. Gib was trying to say as how he'd always thought that renting was something you did by the month, and leasing was when you wanted to keep something for a longer spell. But then Livy interrupted and with that dangerous, too-innocent look on her face she said, "Well, I guess farm-outs are leased then, because you get to keep them till they're eighteen."

So Gib thought he knew why he was back at the Rocking M, at least as far as Livy was concerned, but the next day she was extra nice to him, like always after she'd had a spell of being real ornery.

Gib had been back at the Rocking M for almost a week, and he was still wondering about why he was there when, on a cold, clear November day, something happened that definitely gave him something else to ponder on.

Chapter 6

————◆◆◆————

By Saturday morning the blizzard finally blew itself out. The heavy clouds disappeared and a weak, wintry sun shone down on a gleaming white ocean of snow. A smooth and level ocean out on the open prairie, but one that piled up in deep white waves around fences and buildings.

On the windward side of the house and barn the snow was as high as Gib's head but in the open barnyard it was spread smooth and thin as a white carpet. And it was on that sleek white carpet that Gib rode Silky for the first time since his return to the Rocking M.

He'd asked permission at breakfast that morning and Missus Julia had asked Hy if he thought it would be all right. Hy was planning to take advantage of the settled weather to drive the team into Longford for supplies, but when Gib asked he said, "Don't see why not. You'll not be needin' my help. She'll be feeling her oats, that's for certain, but you'll know how to keep the lid on her till she settles down. Won't you, Gibby?"

So then Missus Julia said to be sure to bundle up, and Miss Hooper found him an old train engineer's cap with woolly ear flaps. Livy hadn't said anything at all at the table; in fact she didn't even seem to be listening. But when Gib, bundled up like a North Pole Eskimo, was going out the door, there she was dressed up in her coat and boots and wearing a new fur-trimmed bonnet.

"I'm coming too," she said, and when Gib stared at her in consternation, wondering what to say, she went on, "Don't worry. I won't ask to ride. I just want to watch." And then when Gib went on staring she added angrily, "I have permission. Don't you believe me? Want to come back inside and ask my mother?"

Gib shook his head. "No, I believe you. I just thought . . ."

"Yes, I know what you're thinking. You're thinking that the last time I rode Silky you got sent away. Well, don't worry. Nobody's going to send you away again." Then her blue eyes widened and in an innocent, little-girl voice she said, "At least not till you're eighteen."

Gib had never gotten angry easily but when someone, like old Elmer back in the orphanage, went out of their way to do or say something ornery, Gib always felt it deep down in the bottom of his stomach. Once or twice he'd even punched somebody for that kind of meanness, but that

42

somebody had never been a lot smaller than he was, and a girl at that. Gib unclenched his fists and took a deep breath. Then he took hold of Livy by both shoulders and said very slowly, "Look here, Livy Thornton. Don't you go making any more remarks about farm-outs, 'cause if you do—if you do . . ."

He stopped then, noticing that Livy's eyes and mouth were wide open and her breath was coming in little shaky gasps. She looked downright terrified. Suddenly Gib felt a grin coming on. " 'Cause if you do," he repeated, "I'm going to dump you in a snowdrift—headfirst."

He turned her loose then and headed for the barn, wondering what she'd do to get even. Wondering, but not regretting what he'd done, nor even looking back, so he didn't notice she was right behind him until he was inside the barn. He was on his way to the tack room when something made him turn and there she stood, right across from Silky's stall. When he stopped to stare, she smiled and nodded as if he'd just paid her a nice compliment instead of threatening to dump her in a snowdrift.

"Yes," she said, smiling sweetly, "I'm still here."

Gib shook his head in amazement. He was still feeling pretty flabbergasted as he took down his tack and headed back toward the stall.

But then there was Silky to think about. She greeted him with her usual gentle nicker and nodded her head in appreciation when he started in with the currycomb. And later when he brought in the bridle she held her head down low and almost reached for the bit.

"Just look at you taking the bit like that," Gib whispered. "I know what you're telling me. You're saying that you surely are itching to stretch your legs a little." When the saddle went on she didn't even hump her back against the tightening of the cinch, but when he opened the stall door she snorted a bit and began to step sideways.

Gib had almost forgotten about Livy until he heard someone say, "She looks excited, doesn't she?" and sure enough, there she was. Livy was looking pretty excited herself. Prancing along in her shiny boots, tossing her curly head and rolling her big eyes so that the whites showed.

"Yep." Gib grinned. " 'Pears to be quite a lot of excitement around here. So now we'll see who's going to be too excited to listen to reason."

Outside the barn in the cold, crisp sunshine Silky skittered a bit when Gib swung himself up into the saddle, but once he was on board and the reins were talking, she settled down some. And when he put her to walking around and around the snow-swept barnyard, she didn't even dance. But Gib could feel how her slow, tiptoeing walk had dancing right there under the surface. And running was there too. The hot-blooded burning urge to run full out and free, across the open prairie.

So he kept her walking until her hoofprints had turned the pure white snow of the barnyard into a horseshoe-patterned carpet. And then went on walking some more, even though Livy, watching from just outside the barn door, was obviously getting impatient. Clapping her hands and stomping her feet against the cold, she called out advice now and then. "Why don't you let her out just a little?" she yelled once, and a little later, "This is getting boring. Let her stretch her legs a little."

But Gib only grinned and nodded, and it wasn't until they'd been around the barnyard maybe fifteen or twenty times that he loosened the reins. Immediately Silky came up against the bit with an excited snort, but when he let her know that a trot was all he was asking for, she reluctantly quieted down with only an occasional head-tossing, tail-swishing, sidestepping flourish to let him know how she was feeling.

They'd moved on to a slow, controlled lope before Gib realized that his audience had grown some. A stranger, a large man wearing a big Stetson and fancy fringed and silver-mounted chaps, was right there at the edge of the barnyard, sitting on a rangy, Roman-nosed buckskin. Just sitting there quietly as if he'd been there for quite a spell.

Gib recognized the horse right off. Way back last winter someone had ridden that same buckskin to one of the Thorntons' dinner parties. Gib remembered taking the winded, lathered-up gelding to the barn and cooling him off a little before putting him in an empty stall. He'd had to go back out then to take care of some other guests' riding and buggy horses, but when everyone had arrived he went back to the barn and rubbed the buckskin down and gave him a few swallows of water and a small flake of hay. Gib grinned, remembering how the Roman-nosed rascal had thanked him for his trouble by trying to nip him.

Gib remembered the horse for certain. He wasn't all that sure about the man, but that wasn't too surprising. That big old Stetson was sitting so low there wasn't much face showing under it. And truth to tell, Gib had always been better at remembering horses than people.

Trying to tip his hat before he remembered that Miss Hooper had strapped the earflaps down under his chin, Gib settled for a wave. "Howdy, mister," he called. "Did you want to see Mrs. Thornton?"

The man touched his spurs to the buckskin's flanks and came on into the barnyard. Close up his bony, thin-lipped face did look a mite familiar. "You looking to see Mrs. Thornton?" Gib repeated. But instead of answering Gib's question the stranger only went on staring at Silky.

"So that's the Thornton Thoroughbred, is it?" he asked. "The one who caused Mrs. Thornton's injury?"

Surprised, Gib gulped a little before he said, "Yes, sir. Yes, she did, but it wasn't her—"

"Who's been handling her?" the man interrupted.

"Handling her?" Gib asked.

"Yes. Who's been settling her down?" The man sounded

46

impatient. "I've heard she used to be a real fireball. Who's been taking the mischief out of her?"

Before Gib could decide how to answer, another voice said, "Gib's been training her." And there Livy was again, standing just a few feet away.

The stranger turned and tipped his Stetson. "Well, hello there, little neighbor lady," he said. "Perhaps you don't remember me, but I remember you. Met you more than once a few years back when . . ."

"I know you, Mr. Morrison," Livy said politely. Too politely, Gib thought anxiously. "I remember you quite well."

Gib glanced quickly from Livy to the stranger and back again. He had a feeling that something was going on that wasn't being put into words, but he had an even stronger feeling that it might be said real soon. And, judging by the look on Livy's face, he couldn't help wondering how neighborly those words were going to be.

He was still wondering when the man swung down off the buckskin. "Well, I'm glad to hear that you remember me, Miss Thornton," he said. And then, to Gib, "I'll leave the buckskin at the rack for the moment, but I'd like you to put him in the barn as soon as you finish with the mare. I won't be long, so you needn't unsaddle him. Just put him in out of the wind."

As the man called Morrison headed for the hitching rack, both Gib and Livy watched him go in silence. It was a tense, edgy silence that lasted for a minute or so before Gib asked, "Morrison?" He knew he'd heard the name before. "You say his name is Morrison? Isn't he the one who . . . ?"

Livy's face looked dangerous. Not sugarcoated, sneaky dangerous this time. More like out-and-out ready to bite and kick. "Yes," she said between her teeth. "The Mr. Morrison who stole my mother's ranch."

Chapter 7

————◆◆◆◆————

Morrison. Gib remembered now. It had been Hy who'd told him that when Mr. Thornton sold off most of the Rocking M's land the buyer had been a man named Clark Morrison. A man who, according to Hy, had more money than sense. But Hy hadn't said anything about stealing, at least not as far as Gib could recollect.

Jumping down off Silky, Gib asked Livy what she meant about stealing. But there was no answer. After a moment he asked again. And then, "Livy? Livy?" Still no answer. Instead she just went on staring toward the house through narrowed eyes. It wasn't until he whispered, "Did you say he stole your mother's ranch?" that she finally answered.

"Yes, stole. Come on. Let's go see what he wants now." But when Gib pointed out that, first off, he had to take care of Silky, and then the buckskin as well, she sighed impatiently. "Well, go ahead then. But I'm going in now. I've got to find out why he's here."

Even though Gib was hurrying all he could, it was nearly half an hour before the two horses were taken care of and he was free to head for the house. Leaving his coat and boots in the storm porch, he went down the hall in his stocking feet. The house seemed quiet and deserted. He was tiptoeing, halfway to the staircase, when something hit him. A hard and sharp whack, it was, right on his shinbone. Came near to scaring the wits out of him.

He'd jumped sideways like a spooked horse, thinking rattlesnake, or maybe a bear trap, before he saw that what had hit him was nothing but a bootjack. A bootjack with Livy Thornton on the other end of it.

Crouched down under the coatrack, halfway invisible among all the long winter overcoats, Livy was still holding the weapon she'd used to get Gib's attention. But now she put it down and, with her finger to her lips, she grabbed Gib's sleeve with her other hand and tugged him down the hall toward the parlor.

"In there," she mouthed as they passed the library. "Morrison and Hoop and my mother. I've been listening to them."

"Listening?" Gib asked, once they were safely inside the parlor.

Livy nodded. "Yes, listening. The door wasn't quite shut and I could hear almost everything they said."

"Yeah?"

"Yes." Livy sounded pleased with herself. "Especially everything *he* said. He was the loudest."

"So, what did he say?"

She shrugged. "Oh, well, what he actually talked about was the weather, and if there was anything he could do to help, and things like that. But that wasn't really what he was thinking about. I could tell. I mean—" Livy grabbed the front of Gib's shirt and shook it. "I mean I could tell what he was really thinking about was how he could get the rest of our land. And the house too. I think he really wants our house."

Gib was still wondering how Livy could tell what a person was thinking when he was talking about something else, when she suddenly pushed him back behind the door. "Shhh," she said. "Here he comes. Stay there."

She disappeared then, leaving Gib behind the open door feeling like a sneak thief, or at least like somebody who was about to be in a whole lot of trouble.

Someone was coming, all right. The library door creaked and voices and footsteps came down the hall. A man's voice and then Miss Hooper's. When the voices and footsteps passed without stopping, Gib relaxed enough to see the funny side of the fix he was in. He smiled ruefully. He'd sure enough let Livy set him up again. This time she'd stuck him behind the door in his stocking feet, listening in on things he probably had no business hearing, while she herself disappeared to God knew where.

He could hear Miss Hooper's voice clearly now. "Thanks again for stopping by, and for your kind offer," she was saying. "But as you see, we're doing quite well, at least for the present. On days like this Hy can get into town with the team, and we do have the telephone, at least when it chooses to work."

"Yes indeed," the man's voice answered. "But if there's anything I can do, just let me know. Still no telephone line out our way, of course, but you could send the boy over and I'd be glad to—"

"The boy? Oh, you're referring to Gibson?"

Gib felt himself quiver like a stretched rope. "Gibson, is it?" Morrison said. "Ah, yes. The Whittaker orphan." A pause. "Was it Gibson who was exercising the black mare this morning?"

"Yes. Yes, it was," Miss Hooper said, and then, "He's probably still out in the barn. Shall I ask him to bring your horse around?"

For a frozen second Gib wondered what he'd do if Miss Hooper went looking for him, leaving Mr. Morrison right there outside the parlor door. But then, to his great relief, he heard the man say, "Never mind calling the boy. I'll go out to the barn myself. Give me another chance to admire that good-looking Kentucky-bred of Mrs. Thornton's." They were almost out of earshot by then but when the front door opened and the cold air rushed in it carried Morrison's voice as he was saying how beautiful something was. "Beautiful, absolutely beautiful," his exact words were, and then something more. Something that made Gib catch his breath in dismay. A question about a *sale*. About whether Mrs. Thornton would "consider a sale?"

Even though Gib stretched his ears till they nearly fell off he couldn't make out how Miss Hooper answered. He was still behind the parlor door with his ear pressed to the crack when the front door shut with a bang and Miss Hooper's footsteps came back down the hall and turned into the library. Gib was pressed back against the wall, trying to remember exactly what he'd heard, when Livy suddenly reappeared.

"You can come out now," she said, peering around the door. "They've gone."

Gib sighed. He looked around the room. "Hey," he asked, "where were you? Where were you hiding?"

"Oh, I wasn't hiding," Livy said. "At least not exactly. I was lying there on the sofa pretending to be asleep." She giggled. "If they'd looked in they would have just said, 'Oh, look at that. She's taking a nap. Isn't that sweet.' "

Gib couldn't help smiling, but then his grin faded. "Did you hear them? Did you hear what that man was asking Miss Hooper just as he went out the door?" he asked.

Livy nodded grimly. "Yes, I did. What did I tell you? He wants to get the rest of our land."

"Land?" Gib was puzzled. He'd been sure Morrison had been talking about Black Silk. There was no time to argue the point, and for that matter, no reason to. As he knew from experience, arguing with Livy never got you anywhere. Insisting they'd been talking about Silky when Livy was sure it was the ranch would be just like insisting on Patrick Henry instead of Paul Revere. And this time he wouldn't dare ask Miss Hooper to settle the argument. As they entered the kitchen Livy ran to the window that faced the driveway.

"He's coming," she whispered. "I hear him. See, there he goes."

Gib stayed where he was until the pounding of hoofbeats and the jingling of tack faded away. When she turned from the window Livy was frowning fiercely. "About Morrison stealing your mother's ranch—?" Gib started to say, when she ran right past him and out of the room.

Gib sighed and shrugged. He really needed to talk to somebody. Hy might have been able to help but he was in Longford. Miss Hooper and Mrs. Thornton were still in the library and Mrs. Perry seemed to have disappeared. He waited around in the kitchen for several minutes before he gave up and headed back out to the barn, where there were better things to do than worry about questions that never got answered.

It was a good time to get some shoveling done. That way Comet and Caesar could come home to spanking-clean stalls. And probably Silky could use a good grooming too. Actually, the way it turned out, it was Silky herself who got most of the attention.

She needed it, Gib decided. Earlier there hadn't been time to give her much more than a lick and a promise what with trying to hurry and having Morrison's buckskin to deal with. But as Gib curried and brushed, his mind kept going back to Morrison and what he'd said about whether Mrs. Thornton would consider a sale.

She wouldn't, he was sure. Well, almost sure. After all, if she'd refused to sell Silky when her husband wanted her to after the accident, surely she wouldn't do it now when she was the only one who had any say-so.

"No, she never would," Gib told Silky as he brushed her forelock. "Like Hy says, Mrs. Thornton's a real prairie-bred Merrill, and no Merrill would give up owning the most beautiful horse in the whole world. Now, would they?" Silky nodded her head and then shook it violently. The shaking surely did mess up her forelock, but Gib only chuckled. "You tell 'em, Silky," he said. "Course she wouldn't. Never in a million years."

Chapter 8

———◆◆◆———

A couple of days later the same old unanswered questions were still hanging around. Hy wasn't any help whatsoever. The damp, chilly weather had set his broken bones to aching, which always made him silent and extra ornery. So when Gib started in, once or twice, by asking if Hy thought Mrs. Thornton would ever sell Silky, all he got was a snort and a growling "Not likely, but you never know."

Miss Hooper was no help either. Not because she wasn't talking but because it wasn't easy to find her alone. In fact, looking to find a moment alone with Miss Hooper put Gib in mind of how hard it had been to find a minute to talk to Miss Mooney way back when he'd been a junior orphan and there were thirty other juniors trying to horn in on the conversation.

There'd been one chance on Monday morning when Gib

reported to the library a little early. Miss Hooper was already at the table but there was no sign of Livy. Gib hurriedly pulled out his chair, sat down—and then waited. Miss Hooper was reading a book by Ralph Waldo Emerson.

Gib waited impatiently, glancing now and then at the door, where Livy would be appearing at any moment. But the reading went on and on. After a minute or two Gib cleared his throat and began, "Miss Hooper. Miss Hooper, could I ask a question?"

"Yes, what is it?" Miss Hooper was holding her place with one finger and looking impatient.

"Miss Hooper, Livy says that Mr. Morrison wants to buy the rest of the Rocking M land." He thought about adding "And Black Silk too," but he only said, "And the house. Livy says he wants to buy this house too."

Miss Hooper was the only person Gib knew who could look amused and angry at the same time. "And so what's the question, boy?" she asked. "That astounding bit of information sounded more like a statement than a question. Are you asking me if it's true? Is that it?"

Gib nodded. "Yes, ma'am. I guess that's what I'm asking, all right."

But at that very moment the library door slammed open with a loud bang and Livy rushed in, chattering excitedly. "Guess what, Gib?" she said. "Guess what I just found out?"

Livy looked from Gib to Miss Hooper and back again. "Well, isn't anyone going to guess?"

This time Miss Hooper's frown looked fairly serious. "No, Miss Thornton," she said. "No one is going to do any guessing, or anything at all, until you go back out and enter this classroom in a more appropriate manner."

For a moment Livy stared back, chin jutting, before she tossed her curls and went out the door. In the moment that passed before she came back in, Miss Hooper said, "I don't know the answer to your question, Gib. I have no idea what that foolish man wants to do."

By then Livy was back again. Pacing slowly to the table, she curtsied to Miss Hooper with exaggerated dignity before she pulled out her chair, sat, and patted down her skirt. Then she turned to Gib and said, "Never mind guessing. I'll tell you. Tomorrow you're going to drive me to Longford School." She paused, glanced at Miss Hooper, and added, "Tomorrow I'm going to start going to a real school again, and Gib's going to go too. I just heard my mother talking to Hy about it."

Miss Hooper's lesson that day was about Ralph Waldo Emerson and the transcendentalists, but afterward Gib didn't remember a whole lot about it. All the rest of the morning his mind kept slipping off transcendentalism and back onto what Livy had said about going to Longford School.

He'd known it was something he'd have to face up to sooner or later. But now that it was about to happen, there were some questions he would have liked to ask if Miss

Hooper and Livy hadn't been acting like a pair of wet hens. But since they were, he could only try to push his mind in the general direction of transcendentalism and keep his mouth shut. It wasn't until Miss Hooper was dismissing class that she said, "And so, Olivia, I guess Hy and your mother think the weather's going to stay settled long enough to make it worthwhile for you to start in again at the Longford School."

Livy nodded stiffly. "Yes, ma'am," she said with exaggerated, little-girl politeness. "That's what Hy says." Then she picked up her books and marched out of the room.

So that was that, but all afternoon while he was working in the barn and the cowshed Gib's mind was extra busy. There was a lot to think about, like the differences between how things had been when he was at the Rocking M before and how they were now.

All last school year, for instance, while Mr. Thornton had taken Livy to the Longford School every day on his way to the bank, Gib had only been allowed to study with Miss Hooper. And only then if he'd finished all his work in the barnyard. And now he was to go to school too. Which a body might take to mean he was no longer just a farm-out. "Or then again," he told Silky while he was picking her hooves, "it just might mean that Livy needs someone to drive the team."

But there were other thoughts that pestered Gib all that afternoon, churning out of the dark corners of his mind like small dark twisters. Thoughts about how he was going to like being at Longford School. At a school where, like as not, he'd be the only orphan farm-out.

Gib slapped Silky's flank to make her move over so he could get to her right hind foot. The slap was harder than he'd meant it to be and Silky snorted accusingly. But Gib only snorted back impatiently and jerked her hoof up off the ground. "They'll all know what I am," he said between clenched teeth. "And even if they don't know right off, Livy's bound to tell them."

In bed that night Gib thought a lot about Longford School. Scenes kept cropping up in his mind. Clear, vivid scenes like the ones he used to have in his dreams about the future, except that there wasn't anything very hopeful about these particular imaginings. Most of them were about things like walking into a classroom where a lot of boys, and girls too, he reminded himself, would be staring at him. The thought of being stared at by girls was particularly troublesome to someone who'd grown up in a Home for Boys, where you didn't get much practice at that kind of thing.

And Livy would be there too, of course, saying things like "This is Gibson Whittaker, the orphan farm-out who works for us." It was, he told himself, the kind of thing Livy was sure to say.

Chapter 9

⸻❖⸻

The weather was fine that day, cold and nippy but with a hazy sun shining in a cloudless sky. A sky that sat over the snowy prairie like an enormous blue hat edged in white where it met the snowy horizon. Livy was wearing her warmest coat and the new fur-trimmed bonnet, and Gib was pretty bundled up too. And during that long ride Livy was extra nice, at least most of the time.

The only time Livy wasn't exactly friendly was when Gib brought up the subject of Morrison. He started out by saying he'd heard that Mr. Morrison had bought a lot of land from her father, all right. "But nobody said anything about stealing. What did you mean when you said he stole your mother's land?"

"What did I mean?" Livy's voice cracked like a whip. "I mean he stole it. When you get something away from someone who doesn't want to sell it, it's stealing, isn't it?"

She put her mittened hands up over her face and held them there for quite a while before she jerked them away and said, "Besides, I don't want to talk about it."

So Gib changed the subject by talking about horses, which usually got Livy's attention. He began by asking Livy if she'd ever noticed how he tapped Comet with the whip once in a while. Comet but not Caesar.

"Yes," Livy said, "I noticed. My father did that too. I thought he just hated Comet the most. Why do you do it?"

Gib chuckled. " 'Cause Comet needs it. A body might expect a matched pair like those two to behave about the same. But they're just about as different as can be. For instance, look how Caesar is always right up there into the collar, working hard. But old Comet just lays back and loafs unless you tap him with the whip now and then, just enough to keep his mind on what he's supposed to be doing. But Caesar's no angel. He's the one who'll try to take a nip out of you while you're cleaning his stall. And Comet never bites, or kicks either. You can crawl right under Comet's belly without him batting an eye."

Livy seemed really interested. She asked a lot of questions and wanted to be the one who tapped Comet the next time he needed it. After that, even when the topic of conversation changed from horses to school, it went on being pretty friendly.

Gib liked the weather and driving the team, and what he

really liked was when Livy went out of her way to tell him some things he needed to know about going to Longford School. About Miss Elders, the upper grades' teacher, and how strict she was about whispering in class. And which boys were the meanest.

"Rodney is the worst," Livy said. "Or else maybe Alvin. But they're both mean as sin, and they just love getting other people into trouble." She looked over at Gib for a moment before she went on, "They have tricks they like to play on people. On new people especially. Things like putting toads in your lunch bucket. Alvin put a toad in my lunch bucket once and when I opened it I screamed my head off. Rodney told me who did it, so I told on Alvin and he had to write a long essay about toads, and another one about being a good citizen. Only I got scolded too, for screaming in the classroom and for tattling. Miss Elders doesn't hold with tattling."

"Thanks for the warning." Gib chuckled. "Don't care much for toads myself. 'Specially if they're sitting on my sandwich."

Livy giggled. "Did the boys at the Lovell House school do mean things like that to each other?" she asked.

"At school?" Gib shook his head. "Don't recollect much meanness going on during classes. . . ." Then he remembered how Elmer Lewis had written a dirty word on his spelling paper and gotten him sent to the Repentance Room, and he told Livy.

"The Repentance Room?" Livy asked eagerly. "That sounds terrible. Tell about the Repentance Room."

So Gib started in on how, when you got into trouble at Lovell House, you got locked up in a little closet way up on the top floor. And how you had to miss dinner and stay there till after bedtime. Livy listened big-eyed and slack-jawed, and when he finished she asked a lot of questions and giggled some when Gib tried to make the whole thing sound sort of ridiculous, which it really was when you thought about it from a distance. From a good big distance.

Livy looked pretty horrified when he told how cold it had been, and how he'd worried that they might forget about coming to let him out. So he kind of made a joke out of how he'd wondered if they'd be sorry when they found his poor old skeleton. "Yep, nothing but a poor old skeleton messing up the Repentance Room floor." Gib chuckled, and after a moment Livy laughed too.

The ride went real fast. Gib was surprised how soon they topped the last little rise and there, up ahead, was the schoolhouse. When Gib reined the team to a stop in front of Longford School, Livy was pointing and bouncing around on the buggy seat. "See, there it is," she was saying. "Longford Elementary School." Just ahead of them a short lane led to a two-story stone building with two big chimneys and two smaller ones, and lots of tall, narrow windows.

Gib chuckled. "Yep, I see it. Didn't know you were that crazy about schooling."

"Oh, I'm not," she said. "I just like seeing everybody again. All my friends and . . ." Without even finishing what she was saying, she suddenly jumped out of the buggy and took off down the lane at a run, waving her hand at two girls who were going up the front steps of the schoolhouse. Gib watched for a moment before he clucked the team into a trot and headed for Appleton's Livery Stable.

There was, Hy had told him, a leaky old stable out behind the schoolhouse. According to Hy, a few students from nearby farms left their critters in the stable's dirty old tie stalls during the school day. Mostly plow horses and a donkey or two, Hy said. But Missus Julia didn't want her horses kept there. So Gib was to go on in to Appleton's Livery Stable, where they'd always been kept when Mr. Thornton drove to the bank every day. "But don't you wait to unhitch them," Hy said. "Just turn them over to old Ernie and hike back to the school. Won't take you more'n fifteen minutes or so."

So Gib found Ernie, the old man who worked as a stable boy, turned the team over to him, and started hiking. Stepped right along too, for more reasons than one. He didn't want to be late on his first day, for one thing, and for another, keeping his mind on hurrying kept him from thinking about what might be going to happen once he got where he was going. And also from thinking about how Livy, after being so friendly in the buggy, had dashed off to see some school friends without even saying good-bye. And without waiting to answer some important questions that Gib hadn't gotten around to asking. Questions like where he should go once he was inside the building.

He was almost to the schoolhouse steps when his hurrying feet wavered and, for a second, came to a dead stop. From up on the buggy's seat the schoolhouse hadn't brought anything in particular to mind. But now, staring straight up at the stone building, something dark and painful swarmed up into his memory, reminding him of his first glimpse of another tall gray building. His first glimpse of Lovell House Home for Orphaned and Abandoned Boys, way back when he was only six years old.

Gib gasped and swallowed hard. He was mighty close to heading back down the stairs when the door opened and a young woman looked out. She smiled at Gib and asked, "New boy?" and when he nodded she went on asking questions. "Miss Elders's class?" After another nod from Gib she said, "Thought so. Living at the Rocking M, aren't you?" Gib nodded. "First door on your left. And hurry along." Pointing to the bell rope that hung down from the tower, she added, "I'll give you ten seconds."

Gib hurried. When he reached the first door on his left he stopped, took a deep breath, stepped inside, and found himself in a roomful of activity. Boys and girls were coming out of the cloakroom, hurrying up the aisle, and taking their seats. But then, only a few seconds later, at the first loud clang of the bell, there was a sudden silence. The whole class, about twenty fifth- and sixth-graders, settled into their seats. And as the bell went on clanging, they turned, one by one, to look at Gib where he was still standing just inside the door. Feeling the embarrassing red warmth spreading up his face, Gib looked down at his boots.

Somebody giggled. There was another giggle, and then a louder, mean-sounding laugh that ended as suddenly as it began, drowned out by a loud rapping noise. Gib went on looking at his boots for a while longer before he managed to look up out of the tops of his eyes.

A tall, slender woman wearing a dark skirt and white blouse and a no-nonsense frown was standing in front of the room. As Gib watched she rapped on her desk again with a long wooden pointer. The silence deepened.

"Boys and girls," Miss Elders said, "I'd like you to meet your new fellow student . . ." She looked down at a paper on her desk. "Your fellow student Gibson Whittaker. Please tell Gibson hello, and then get out your readers. And Gibson, take the empty desk there on your left."

The hellos were loud and soft, and they came with friendly smiles, blank stares, and mean, sarcastic grins. Among the blank-eyed faces there was, near the front of the room, a familiar one, surrounded by yellow-brown curls. Familiar but not particularly welcoming. Among her Longford friends Livy, it seemed, had other fish to fry.

Trying to return the greetings, Gib stretched his lips in a counterfeit grin before he folded his long legs under a smallish desk and began one of the longest days he'd ever spent.

Chapter 10

That night, back in his own room, Gib closed the door firmly and got into bed. But the door to his mind, the door that let in unwelcome recollections, was harder to close.

Classroom recollections kept sneaking in. The constant curious stares that were there whether the new boy was trying to answer a question about the U.S. Constitution or just working quietly on long division. Some of the stares might have been just curiosity, but there were others that were downright mean. And the note that somebody put in his lunch pail was even meaner. A note that said, "Hey, orfan. Hope you like to fight." There was no signature.

Nothing much more than stares and notes went on in the classroom. Miss Elders saw to that. But once in a while some other things happened. A push or two and a tripping attempt when someone, probably Rodney, or else Alvin, stuck out a foot as Gib was walking down the aisle.

Gib had met Rodney and Alvin, all right, and they were as bad as Livy said they were. Rodney was big and heavyset with a sharp-boned face that might have been good-looking if it weren't for his squinty, snake-eyed stare. Looked like a city slicker, Gib thought. A city slicker dressed up in flashy store-bought clothes and patent leather shoes. His pal, Alvin, was taller and not as well turned out. Alvin was wearing a cowhide vest and big, scuffed-up boots. With his woolly reddish hair and ornery stare, he put Gib in mind of a bad-natured Hereford bull. Gib could see, right off, that the two of them weren't going to be a bit friendly, but during the noon recess a couple of other people were. One of the friendly ones was a boy named Graham, who stopped by Gib's desk to tell him about lunch recess.

The noon hour, Graham told Gib, was the best part of the day. In the fall and spring you could play games in the school yard, and even when you had to stay in because of bad weather you were allowed to do what Miss Elders called "civilized socializing." Which simply meant visiting with friends. As long as it was very quiet socializing, Graham said.

That sounded fine to Gib. So after he'd finished the lunch Mrs. Perry had packed for him, he looked around for someone to socialize with. But Livy was real busy talking to a bunch of her girlfriends and Graham was back at his desk reading a book. Gib didn't feel like horning in on any of the other socializers, so he put on his mackinaw and went outside. But that didn't last long either. The snow-covered playground was deserted, not to mention freezing cold.

Back in the classroom Miss Elders was at her desk correcting some papers, and everything was pretty quiet and orderly. Gib put away his mackinaw and sat down at his desk with a history book. He read a little, but mostly he watched and listened. He didn't hear much, though, because people kept their voices down. The bunch of girls standing around Livy's desk even managed to giggle quietly. The noontime recess was more than half over when Bertie Jameson came over to Gib's desk and started talking about Josephine.

Bertie was a scrawny little fifth-grader who talked so softly that Gib only got about half of what he was saying, but after a while he made out that Josephine was probably Bertie's riding horse.

"Come out to the stable with me and I'll let you see her," Bertie whispered. Gib had been wanting to see the schoolhouse stable, so he got into his mackinaw again and out they went. The stable was maybe a hundred yards from the schoolhouse and it looked and smelled pretty bad, all right; just a row of muddy tie stalls under a saggy roof. Two of the stalls were occupied by donkeys and in the third was an enormous dirty brown critter that turned out to be Josephine.

Gib's guess was about right. Josephine was what you might call a riding horse if you weren't too particular. A huge old swaybacked mare, she was rawboned and Roman-nosed, with a skimpy mane and tail and such out-sized hooves that you had to figure there'd been a Clydesdale somewhere in her family tree. But Bertie insisted that she was fast as a Thoroughbred. "And she's a real good foul-weather horse too," he whispered eagerly. "Me and Josephine got here every day during the blizzard last week. You should ought to see how she plows right through them three-foot drifts like they warn't there 'tall."

Gib could believe it. He thought of saying that hooves that big must be almost as good as snowshoes. But he didn't because he was afraid Bertie might think he was making fun of Josephine.

Bertie was still fussing over his big mare, moving her to another stall that wasn't quite as muddy, when Gib decided to head back to the schoolroom. And that was when the trouble began. Rodney and his buddy, Alvin, were waiting just outside the stable, and when Gib came around the corner they stepped in front of him, blocking his path. Rodney's mouth was stretched into an angry-dog grin. "Howdy there, orphan," he snarled. "You get my note?"

Gib's heart did an extra beat or two but he tried to ignore it. He knew what Rodney and Alvin were up to. One thing

72

you learned early on in a Home for Boys was what a bully looked like. And also how to spoil their fun by not letting them see how scared you were.

Taking a deep breath, Gib grinned back. Not a "dare you" grin but a slow, easy one. "Note?" he asked. "You wrote that note in my lunch pail?"

"Yeah," Rodney said. "I wrote it."

Gib nodded slowly before he reached into his pocket and pulled out the wrinkled scrap of paper. A scrap on which someone had written "Hey, orfan. Hope you like to fight." Unfolding it carefully, he studied it for a moment before he said, "You wrote this here note that says, 'Howdy Gibson Whittaker. Welcome to Longford School'?"

Rodney's angry glare changed to confusion. He was reaching out to take the note out of Gib's hand when the sound of running feet made him whirl around. All three of them turned just in time to see Bertie Jameson dash out from the other end of the stable and head for the schoolhouse steps at a dead run. Bertie was obviously a fast runner, skimming over the icy ground like a water bug on a pond. It occurred to Gib that scrawny little boys like Bertie who had classmates like Rodney and Alvin probably learned to be fast runners in order to stay alive.

Grabbing hold of Gib's coat, Rodney yelled, "Catch him, Al." Bowlegged old Alvin gave it a try. But Bertie had a good head start, and after a short dash and two or three stumbles on the icy snow, Alvin gave up and came panting back.

"Never mind." Rodney was still holding on to the front of Gib's mackinaw. "We got this one."

Alvin looked uneasy. "But Bertie's going to tell," he said. "He's going to go in there and tell Miss Elders."

"Naw, he won't," Rodney said. "Bertie knows better than to tell on me." Turning back to Gib, Rodney went on, "You hear me, orphan. Nobody tells on Rodney Martin if they know what's good for them. You hear me?" He jerked Gib toward him with one hand and swung his other fist, hard and fast, right at Gib's face.

But Gib saw it coming. Ducking his head, he butted it into Rodney's chest, grabbed him with both arms, and shoved hard. Gib had done his share of shoveling and hoeing and had the strong arm muscles to prove it. So when he grabbed and held on, Rodney had a hard time shaking him loose. A split second later the two of them were rolling around on the icy ground.

The rolling lasted for quite a while without much damage being done. Rodney kept trying to use his fists, but with Gib plastered to his chest there wasn't much room for a backswing. The few punches he managed to land didn't hurt Gib all that much. But then Alvin got in on the action.

He'd been prancing around Gib and Rodney for quite a

while, yelling things like "Hit him, Rod. Hit the dirty farm-out." And Rodney had gone on trying to, without much success. But then Alvin stopped yelling and started kicking.

The first kick hit Gib in the ribs. It hurt real bad and, for a second or two, pretty near knocked the breath clean out of him. He was still holding on, struggling to breathe and closing his eyes against the pain, when a second kick hit his left leg up near the thigh. That one hurt too.

But then, just as Gib was beginning to feel pretty desperate, things started changing. The first change was that Alvin stopped kicking and yelling. Gib was aware of a sudden silence and then a loud metallic noise, a sharp clanging thud, and then another one. And now it was Rodney who was yelling. Right in Gib's ear Rodney was yelling, "Ow. Hey. Stop that."

Another heavy thud, and Rodney yelled again. Suddenly releasing his grip on Gib, he rolled quickly away, and as Gib struggled to his feet he found himself face to face with, of all people, Livy Thornton. A coatless, red-faced Livy whose unbonneted head was a mass of wind-blown curls, and in whose hands was a badly dented lunch bucket. As Gib watched in astonishment Livy walked toward Rodney, swinging the lunch pail by its handle. She missed that time as Rodney, on his feet now, jumped back out of range, but it was easy to tell that she hadn't missed every time. Easy to guess when you saw the dents in her lunch bucket, as well as a bloody cut on Rodney's forehead.

For a moment all four of them stood in a panting, gasping circle, with Rodney holding his forehead and Gib his ribs, while Livy went on clutching her lunch pail. Alvin was in the circle too, jittering around in his big clumsy boots and jumping back out of range when Livy looked in his direction.

"Come on, Gib, let's go in." Livy started back toward the schoolhouse and Gib limped after her. Rodney and Alvin stayed right where they were.

Gib followed as well as he could but because he was limping a little on his left leg and holding his aching ribs, it wasn't easy to keep up. Halfway back to the school building, Livy slowed down and watched him for a moment. "You all right?" she asked.

"Been better. But I'd have been a lot worse if you hadn't showed up." He grinned. "You and that two-barreled lunch bucket."

Livy tossed her head and went on, walking more slowly now. When Gib caught up he asked, "How'd you know what was going on? Did Bertie tell you?"

"No," she said, "he didn't have to. I saw the two of you go out. I knew where you were going. Bertie's always taking people to meet Josephine. I was on my way to the cloakroom to put my pail away when he came running back in looking like . . ." She stopped and made a terrified face, big-eyed and openmouthed. "Bertie didn't say anything to anybody," she said. "But I knew."

They grinned at each other and then laughed out loud. But back in the classroom Livy went straight over to her giggling girlfriends.

Chapter 11

———◆◆◆◆◆———

Lying in bed that night, Gib did a lot of careful tossing and turning while he waited for his mind to shut off and let him go to sleep. Careful tossing because his leg, and especially his ribs, were still remembering Alvin's big old boots. But even though he was feeling tired and sore, nothing, not the ticking clock that kept reminding him how late it was, not even his aches and pains, could keep his mind from shuffling through the things that had happened that day, like a gambler shuffling through a deck of cards.

Some of the memories were pretty painful, but some others weren't, except when they made him laugh. Laughing was out because right at the moment a real hard belly laugh didn't do his ribs any good at all. But even aching ribs couldn't keep him from chuckling a little over what had happened during elocution class.

The bell for the end of lunch hour was still ringing when

Miss Elders started writing on the blackboard. "Elocution Class," she wrote. "Recitations from the Romantic Poets." And after that in large print, "LAST CHANCE!!!"

"Your very last chance," she told the class. Then she paused and added, "Except for Olivia and Gibson, of course. Olivia," she went on, "and you too, Gibson. See me after class for your assignment and we'll expect to hear from you next week."

Then Miss Elders went on to explain that everyone had been given a poem to memorize and recite before the class. Your final grade, she explained to Gib and Livy, would be based not only on how thoroughly you had memorized your material, but also on pronunciation and projection, and most of all on stage presence and dramatic presentation. The four P's, Miss Elders called them—Pronunciation, Projection, stage Presence, and dramatic Presentation. She went on to explain why the four P's were so important when you had any sort of public speaking to do. "As most of you will, at some point in your life," the teacher told the class. Gib's mind wandered for a moment while he considered what kind of public speaking an orphan farmout might be expected to do. But he pricked up his ears in time to listen to Miss Elders tell about how well everyone had done. Nearly everyone, at least.

Actually, Miss Elders said, the recitations had been due last week and nearly everyone had been well prepared. Except for a few people who'd needed more time to complete their memorization, or because they'd forgotten to bring a stage prop they needed for their presentation.

She looked then at a paper on her desk before she said, "Matilda. I trust you've not forgotten your skylark again?"

Matilda Reed, a big blond girl with a twitchy smile, jumped to her feet. "No, Miss Elders. Got it right here." Reaching into her desk, she brought out what looked to Gib like a stuffed crow. Then she scurried to the front of the room and began to recite. Matilda's poem was by a poet named Shelley, and it was a long one. Every time Matilda mentioned the word *skylark* she held the stuffed bird way over her head and gazed up at it.

Gib thought she seemed a bit nervous and jittery, so maybe her grade for stage presence might not be too good, but you had to admit her presentation was mighty dramatic. All the girls and most of the boys clapped like crazy when Matilda finished. Everyone seemed to think that having a stuffed bird as a stage prop was a clever idea, and Gib did too, but he couldn't help wondering if a skylark really did look that much like a crow.

The next recital was by a fifth-grade boy named Jack who waved an American flag while he recited a poem about patriotism by Sir Walter Scott. It was a short poem but Jack's presentation was very dramatic and he got a lot of applause too. The next name Miss Elders called was Rodney Martin.

Gib had been keeping an eye on Rodney during the first two recitations. Slumped down low in his seat, Rodney had been dabbing at his forehead with what looked to be a red-and-white bandanna. But when Miss Elders called his name he quickly stuffed the bandanna into his pocket and got to his feet. Holding his head at a strange angle to kept the right side of his face turned away from the teacher, he walked slowly to the front of the room.

Miss Elders looked at her list and said, "I believe Rodney has chosen to favor us with a recital of 'The Charge of the Light Brigade.' Is that right, Rodney?" With his head still turned sideways, Rodney nodded stiffly and began, " 'The Charge of the Light Brigade' by Alfred, Lord Tennyson." Rodney did have a good loud speaking voice, and he seemed to have the start of his poem pretty well memorized, but he'd hardly gotten to the part about "Cannon to right of them,/Cannon to left of them," when Miss Elders stopped him.

"Rodney," she said sharply, "I'm sorry to interrupt you, but . . ." Hurrying across the room, she took Rodney's chin in her hand and turned his face so that she, and the whole class, could see that a small stream of blood was oozing out of a cut on his forehead and trickling down his right cheek. He was starting to wipe the blood away when Miss Elders caught his arm. "You're really bleeding," she said. "I thought at first that you'd made yourself up to look like a wounded brigadier, but that's real blood, isn't it? What happened to you, Rodney?"

Rodney didn't answer right away. Taking the blood-spotted handkerchief out of his pocket, he dabbed at his forehead. "Nothing. Nothing happened," he finally muttered. "I'm all right."

"What happened, Rodney?" Miss Elders said again in a tone of voice that made the whole class sit up straighter and taller. "You haven't been fighting again, have you? I'm sure you remember what Mr. Shipley said about school-yard fights, and what the punishment would be for repeat offenders. Repeat offenders like yourself, Mr. Martin."

Still holding the handkerchief to his head, Rodney nodded, staring down at the floor and looking so miserable that Gib could almost have felt sorry for him if he hadn't been so worried about what Rodney was going to say about who else had been in the fight.

When Rodney finally looked up his eyes glanced off Livy for only a split second before he mumbled something about walking into a wall.

"A wall. What wall?" Miss Elders asked, and when Rodney only shook his head, she sighed and said, "Well, it seems obvious that this matter will need some looking into. I'll see you after school, Rodney, in Mr. Shipley's office."

Then Rodney went back to his seat, and Miss Elders sent one of the sixth-grade girls to the office to get the first-aid kit. So Rodney's forehead got bandaged, and for the rest of the day he stayed away from Gib, and even farther away from Livy. And there were no more notes either. There were messages, though. Messages that Gib got loud and clear every time he looked in Rodney's direction and caught him looking back. "This isn't over," Rodney's look said. "I'll get you yet, Gib Whittaker."

On the way home in the buggy Gib asked Livy what would happen to Rodney if they found out he'd been fighting, but she only shrugged. "I don't know, and I don't care. But it's bound to be something dreadful because he's always fighting. Like maybe they'll make his parents come to school and talk to the principal. And if that happens his pa will probably beat the tar out of him." She laughed. "But 'e'll never tell who hit him," she said. "Not if they beat him to death." Her giggle had an ornery sound to it. "Rodney Martin would rather die than to have people laughing at him for letting a girl get the best of him."

Gib saw what she meant. "But what if Alvin tells?" he asked.

"He'd never dare," Livy said. "Rodney would kill him."

Gib was pretty sure that was the truth too. Alvin was bigger and taller but Rodney was meaner, and Alvin knew it. And Alvin knew, everybody knew, actually, that life wouldn't be easy for a farm-out nobody that Rodney Martin was looking to beat up on.

Lying there in his bedroom that night, even though it was his own private room, Gib had to accept the fact that he still was one, and that surely was the reason why Rodney was after him. Still a farm-out orphan, and likely to go right on being one for the rest of his life.

Chapter 12

————◆◆◆————

The weather held cold but clear for several days, and Gib and Livy went on driving the team to Longford. Livy said she was glad to be going to a real school again, and she was planning to go right on attending Longford School all the rest of the year.

"Aren't you glad to be going to a real school?" she asked Gib one morning as they were heading down the lane and out onto the Longford road. Gib only shrugged. When Livy pushed him for an answer he said, "Well, far as I can see there are some good things about going to school in Longford, and some bad things."

"Bad? What bad things?" Livy asked. "Don't you like learning all those interesting subjects that Miss Elders teaches about? Like modern writers and elocution?"

So Gib said, "Don't have anything against learning about modern writers, or elocution either. But I wouldn't mind missing out on learning any more about Rodney Martin, for instance. And the other thing is . . ."

He stopped then, not wanting to sound like a whiner. But when Livy told him to go on he said going to school and the time it took to get there were using up a whole lot of daylight. "After the milking and feeding and stall cleaning, there's not much time for Black Silk," he said. "I haven't given her a real good grooming lately and the last time I saddled her up was last Saturday."

Livy only nodded and shrugged, but Gib went on thinking about that last time he'd saddled up Silky and put her through her paces. And how hard it always was to get her to settle down and tend to business when she'd gone so long between workouts.

But even though Gib was sorry to have so little time with Silky, he had to admit he was learning a lot at Longford School. Learning important things about world history and literature and elocution. In fact, he seemed to be making good progress in just about everything except, maybe, "civilized socializing."

Gib didn't mention it to Livy but he'd thought about it quite a bit. Thought and wondered about why socializing, civilized or otherwise, was just about the only subject he wasn't doing very well in. He knew it wasn't that he hadn't tried, but the only people who seemed interested in socializing with an orphan farm-out were Bertie and sometimes Graham. The rest of the students in Miss Elders's fifth and sixth grade found something else to do in a hurry whenever Gib tried to talk to them.

That day, the rest of the way into Longford, Gib went on thinking about socializing. It was being an orphan farm-out that was the problem, he was pretty sure of that. Back at Lovell House he'd always known he could grin at someone and like as not they'd return the favor. Nobody had called it socializing but the fact was he'd done it just fine at Lovell House, where everyone was more or less in the same boat. But at Longford people just looked away. Well, nearly everyone. Not Bertie and Graham and, in a very different way, not Rodney Martin.

The rumor was, according to Livy, that Rodney's pa had pretty near skinned him alive and promised him he'd get it twice as bad if he got in any more fights at school. So Rodney wasn't ready to do any more punching or kicking. Not yet anyway, but he wasn't looking away either. Every time he caught Gib's eye he looked long and hard and showed his teeth in that angry-dog grin he had. Gib knew what that grin meant, all right. What it meant was, "Just you wait, Gib Whittaker." So Gib waited, not having much choice, and while he waited he spent some time wondering what might be going to happen the next time Rodney went on the warpath.

Except for the time it took up, Gib didn't mind driving Caesar and Comet to school every day. He liked driving a team, and he also kind of enjoyed all the talking he and Livy got done during the ride. A lot of the talk was about the team because they were taking turns driving now, and Livy usually had a lot of questions about handling the reins and using them to talk to your team. Gib liked talking to Livy about horses because it was one subject she pretty much let him handle on his own, without a lot of interruptions and arguments.

Another subject that came up a lot was how long it would be before Rodney thought of a way to get even with them both. Livy talked, almost every day, about what Rodney might be planning. "Sooner or later he's bound to go after me for whacking him with my lunch pail," Livy told Gib, "and after you for . . ." She paused then, looking at Gib out of the corners of her eyes and then looking away and getting real busy with the reins.

Gib grinned. "Yeah?" he prompted her. "Get even with me for what? What did I ever do to old Rodney?"

Livy turned to give Gib a long stare. Finally she shrugged and said, "I don't know. For being you, I guess."

Gib grinned. "Can't see how he can blame me for that. Didn't have much say in the matter." His grin faded. "And I didn't exactly choose to be an orphan either."

"What's that got to do with it?" Livy asked.

"Just about everything, far as I can see." Gib chuckled, making out that what he was going to say was some kind of joke. "Guess old Rodney just can't stand being around people who don't belong anywhere."

Livy went on staring but with a different expression on her face. Finally she shook her head and said, "I don't think that's it. You've got it all wrong. I think it's more like he's jealous of you."

"What?" Gib couldn't believe he'd heard right. "What in tarnation—" he started, but at that very second a big old jackrabbit changed the subject. Jumping out onto the road right in front of the team, it spooked Caeser and Comet so badly they tried to make a run for it—in opposite directions. The buggy went off the road to the east and then to the west, and by the time things got back to normal the conversation was back on buggy driving and stayed there all the rest of the way to school. And the next time Gib had a chance to ask Livy what she'd meant she only shrugged and said she didn't remember saying anything about Rodney being jealous.

December was well under way when Hy came down ailing, with a high fever and a whole new batch of aches and pains. Pains that, according to Hy, were "probably just the epizootic and nothin' to worry about." But Miss Hooper said, "Nonsense. Epizootic is a horse ailment. You may think like a horse, Hyram Carter, but you're not quite there yet. What you've got is a bad case of influenza. Human influenza. And if you don't believe me you can just ask Doc Whelan when he gets here."

Right at first Hy said he didn't need a doctor and he

wasn't going to see one, but when Miss Hooper told him the doctor was coming to see Julia anyway Hy said as how he might look in for a minute but not any longer. But by the time Doc Whelan arrived Hy was too sick to do much arguing. So he was put to bed in his upstairs room and the doctor said he wasn't to leave it for at least two full weeks.

Gib was mighty worried about Hy, but what with one thing and another, like getting all the barnyard work done alone in time to get himself and Livy to school, he didn't have much chance to brood about it. All he could do was start the chores at five o'clock in the morning instead of five-thirty and work harder and faster than he ever had in his whole life. Belle, the spotted milk cow, helped out a little by going dry all of a sudden, so there was only grumpy old Bessie to milk. And to Gib's surprise Livy helped out a little too by taking care of the chickens and gathering what few eggs the wintering hens were still producing.

A new storm that had been threatening for several days was still hanging fire on Gib's birthday, the sixteenth of December. There was a birthday party for Gib, just like the one the year before when he turned eleven. Like before, there were presents, a stylish pinstripe suit with long pants from Missus Julia and Miss Hooper, a hand-knit wool scarf from Livy, and a big chocolate birthday cake from Mrs. Perry. As soon as the eating was finished, Gib got sent to his room to try on his new suit and when he came back, everyone made a big fuss over how grand he looked.

Gib had a real good time even though worrying about Hy kind of put a damper on his spirits. Worrying and remembering his last birthday party when Hy had sat right there at the table telling his long-winded stories about the old days when the Rocking M had been one of the biggest ranches in the state. Gib surely did wish he could hear those stories again, right at that very moment.

When Gib's party was over Miss Hooper told him to go with Mrs. Perry when she took some chicken broth up to Hy's room. "Just to cheer him up a little and let him see how handsome you look in your new outfit," Miss Hooper said. So Gib went up to show off his new suit.

Hy was looking bad, pale and shriveled as a worn-out shirt, but he hadn't changed much in some ways. His gravelly voice sounded pretty much the same when he fussed at Mrs. Perry about pestering him with mustard plasters and other such nonsense. And when she pointed out Gib's new suit he managed to grin at Gib and tease him a little about looking like a dude.

"I'd never sign up a gol-durned city slicker like that to ride for any outfit of mine," he said. But then his honking laugh turned into a bad fit of coughing. And all Gib could do was to keep on laughing so as not to let Hy see how worried he was.

In bed that night Gib stayed awake a long time worrying about Hy and then, when his mind began to drift toward sleep, about why he still couldn't get anyone to tell him . . . "To tell me—what?" he asked his sleep-drowned mind. And the only answer was, "What I'm doing here." And the rest of that night, every time he woke up, the question was still right there.

It was on Saturday morning and the light of day was still a long way off when Gib, carrying a kerosene lantern, went down the back steps and headed out across the barnyard through a heavy veil of drifting snow. The storm that had been creeping up on the Rocking M had finally arrived, but this time not with a whoop and a holler. No fierce wind but only a deep mysterious silence and the slow steady drift of fat white flakes. Gib was almost to the barn, and the snowflakes were blending into its whitewashed walls, when something huge and ghostly gray moved into the lantern light. Moved, snorted, and then bolted away into the falling snow.

Chapter 13

Gib stood still, frozen with shock and surprise. He'd seen a horse, he was sure of that. Or almost sure. A huge, pale horse dappled with snowflakes. Or had it been one of his horses? The thought suddenly made him start with alarm. Lightning, perhaps, or one of the bays, their darker hides faded by drifting snow? Jerking open the barn door, he ran inside, turned on the lights, and found everything in order. Heads, bay and roan and shiny black, appeared over stall doors, and soft nickers and impatient stomps greeted his entrance. And at the other end of the corridor the mules, Jack and Diva, were there where they belonged too.

Gib shook his head in amazement. He'd seen a horse. Outside the barn in the predawn darkness he'd surely seen—something. He knew he had. Something that sounded and moved and, now that he thought about it, even smelled like a horse.

He turned back toward the open barn door and stared out into the snow-swept darkness. But nothing moved in the muffled silence. Finally he shrugged and, responding to a chorus of impatient snorts and nickers, said, "All right, all right, you poor starving critters. Here I come."

Climbing up to the loft, he began to send the fat slabs of hay down the chutes into the mangers, Silky's first and then Lightning's. He was breaking the wires on a new bale when Lightning squealed. Not a polite nicker this time, but a loud, challenging whinny. And another whinny answered. Not Silky's familiar call or one of the bays' either. Gib dropped the hay hooks and ran to the ladder.

A strange horse, a big dapple gray, was standing just inside the barn door. Long-legged and well muscled, the gray held his beautiful head high, his eyes wide and white-rimmed with fear. As Gib watched in fascinated wonder the horse minced forward, poised for flight, his ears turning nervously from side to side. He nickered again, more softly now, a call that, to Gib, spoke of fear and hunger. Tiptoeing back to the bale of hay he had just opened, Gib picked up a large flake and headed back toward the ladder.

When the gray saw Gib on the ladder he snorted wildly, halfway reared into a whirling turn, and raced out into the darkness. Gib continued down the ladder, placed the hay on the floor, and moved away, back toward the tack room. He waited then and the horses waited too. Neglecting their hay, they stood at their stall doors, obviously as curious about their strange visitor as Gib was.

Nothing happened. After several minutes Gib decided to finish the feeding, but he left the barn door open just in case. When their oat pans were full the horses went back to their mangers. To them even a gray ghost horse was of less interest than a pan full of oats. Gib was back in the corridor between the stalls, the oat bucket still in his hand, when the visitor suddenly appeared again in the open barn door. Holding his breath, Gib eased back away from the light.

Moving slowly, ears and eyes busy, the gray inched forward. Seeing him more clearly now, Gib could tell that he was not in good condition. Although he was a beautiful animal, a silvery dappled gray with Thoroughbred or maybe Arabian ancestors, he was badly ganted up. His ribs showed under the dappled hide, his long silvery mane was matted and tangled, and strange dark ridges crisscrossed his flanks and withers. When he reached the hay he grabbed a mouthful and then, still chewing, threw up his head to stare wildly around him. Gib let him have a couple more mouthfuls before he began to talk.

Keeping his voice soft and slow, Gib said, "Well, howdy there, stranger," but before he could say any more the gray whirled and ran. But this time he stopped just outside the barn door. Stopped and stared, tossing his head and snorting. Gib went on talking. "No call to run away," he said. "Nothing here that's going to do you any harm. Just lots of good hay." He shook the oat pan. "And oats too. Hear that, boy? Bet you know that sound."

The gray knew the sound all right, and so did the other horses. Silky nickered softly and both she and Lightning appeared again at their stall doors. Gib could see that the presence of the other horses, calm, unfrightened horses, and the sight and smell of food were working on the gray. Still alert and poised for flight, he came back into the barn, began to eat, and went right on eating when Gib, once again, began to talk. So Gib went on telling the gray how beautiful he was in spite of his washboard ribs and dirty hide, and how smart he was to stay right there and eat instead of running off into the snowstorm. But when Gib began to move forward the gray ran again.

This time, while he was gone, Gib opened the door of an empty stall, filled the water pail, moved the hay into the manger, and added a pan of oats. Then he moved back into the shadows near the tack room door, to watch and wait. The gray came back sooner this time, moved to where the hay had been and then, cautiously, stopping and starting nervously, into the open stall. But when Gib crept close enough to shut the door behind him, he went wild. Rearing and kicking the walls, he threatened Gib with bared teeth and flattened ears. But Gib stood his ground just outside the door and went on talking softly.

At last the gray returned to his food, but even while he was eating, the oats first and then the hay, he stopped from time to time to snort and shake his head threateningly, saying, plain as day, what he would do to anyone who pushed him.

It was there under the barn's brighter lights, with the gray no longer facing him, that Gib got a better look at the strange dark stripes that marred the beautiful dappled hide. They were, he could see now, ridges that crisscrossed most of the gray's body, long swollen welts, darkened in places by dried blood. The horse had been, Gib realized with sudden horror, terribly beaten. Not just with a stick or quirt but with something much worse. Probably with something like a bullwhip. Gib had heard of such things. A whip as long as twenty-five feet, that could cut through flesh and even break a man's arm. But to see with his own eyes what it could do to a horse caused a thudding pain in Gib's midsection and a gagging sensation in the back of his throat.

Gib was very late to breakfast that day. He was still taking off his boots when Miss Hooper stuck her head into the storm porch. "Land sakes, boy," she said. "Where have you been? I was just about to bundle up and go looking for you. Delia was sure you'd fallen out of the loft."

Mrs. Perry was standing by the window staring out into the snow, but she threw up her hands and praised the Lord when Miss Hooper announced, "Here he is, Delia. Sound as a dollar." And then to Gib, "But with some explaining to do, young man. Where have you been all this time?"

Gib was ready. It was while he was on his way into the house that he'd stopped to realize that he'd better not tell everything about the gray. Scared and spooky would be all right, he figured. But not angry and out for revenge. Not unless he wanted to stir up a lot of do's and don't's that wouldn't do anything to solve the gray's problem, or Gib's either. So while his story about what had been happening was pretty true as far as it went, it did leave out a few important details.

He'd hardly gotten started when Livy and Missus Julia came in, so he started over again and this time he remembered some things Miss Elders had said about public speaking. Things about projection and stage presence. "It was snowing hard," he said dramatically, "falling almost straight down. Thick and heavy as I've ever seen it. I was almost to the barn when this horse came out of the snow right toward me, looking like a big gray ghost. A big, half-starved dapple gray it was. He was scared and hungry and he let me know right away that he was scared to death and didn't want to be fooled with."

Missus Julia interrupted then to ask if the horse was a wild mustang and Gib told her no. "No, ma'am." He shook his head sharply. "He's hot-blooded, that's for sure," he said, "and he knows about barns and stalls, all right. He's been ridden some too. Got a couple of saddle marks on his

97

back. But he's spookier than a rabbit." He grinned. "Even after I got him into the stall he kept acting real spooky."

"Where is he?" Livy wanted to know. "Where is he now?" And when Gib told her he was right there in the barn shut in one of the extra stalls, she wanted to go see him right at that moment. And she would have too, except her mother told her no.

"Absolutely not," Missus Julia said. "Not until we find out who owns him and where he came from. And Gib, don't you go into the stall with him until Hy says . . ." She stopped then, and they all knew why. There was no telling how soon Hy would be able to tell them anything about the visitor. To tell them just how dangerous the strange intruder was, and what to do with him.

"I'll call Appleton's Livery right after breakfast," Missus Julia said. "That's what I'll do. If he belongs to anyone in our area Mr. Appleton's sure to know about him. And when we find out who his owners are, it will be up to them to come and take care of him."

So they all sat down to one of Mrs. Perry's great breakfasts and while they ate the talk was all about horses. About horses Missus Julia had known when she was a girl and the Rocking M owned dozens of them. All kinds of horses, from raw half-broke mustangs fresh off the open range to hot-blooded aristocrats like Black Silk. Listening to the missus's horse talk, Gib could almost shut his mind to the poor bullwhipped gray, at least for a few seconds at a time.

While they ate and talked the snow went on falling, softly and steadily in fat, wet flakes, piling up smooth and even across the barnyard and out over the open prairie. By the time breakfast was over and Miss Hooper rolled Missus Julia's chair into the library, the phone lines had gone down again. So nobody was going to call Appleton's Livery in Longford or anywhere else. At least not anytime soon.

No one was going to call, or go anywhere either. Watching how quickly the snow filled up the barnyard and the lane that led out to the Longford road, Gib could tell nobody was going to be traveling along that road. No buggy or coach or Model T or anything else on wheels. Standing there at the window watching the snow come down, Gib realized that taking care of the angry gray horse was going to be up to him and him alone.

And he *would* take care of him. Right there, staring out into the falling snow, with his fists clenched and jaw jutting, Gib made himself and the gray a solemn promise. Nothing and nobody was going to keep him from rescuing the poor beaten thing that had drifted in out of the storm looking for safety and a human being he could trust.

Chapter 14

———◆◆◆———

The strange storm went on and on. No fierce winds, and not even any lung-freezing, below-zero cold. Only a steady, stubborn snowfall that appeared to be fixing to go on forever. So much snow that all the buildings at the Rocking M looked to be halfway buried, and a body needed snowshoes just to get from the house to the barn and then on to the cowshed. And in the barn the big gray horse went on telling Gib that he was scared and angry and ready to fight.

The biggest problem was going to be the watering. Gib realized that right away on that first evening as soon as he got out of his snowshoes and hurried down to the gray's stall. Hay was no problem because of the chutes that led down from the loft to each of the mangers, but there was no way to get to the water pail rack without going inside the stall. The gray's water bucket was probably dry as a bone and there didn't look to be much of a chance that Gib was going to be able to do anything about it.

As Gib stood at the door, sizing up the situation, the gray stayed as far away as he could get. If Gib raised his voice or moved too quickly, the big horse snorted fiercely, tossed his head, and pawed the ground.

"I hear what you're telling me," Gib told him. "You're scared and mad as all get-out, and you're going to kick me halfway to Longford if you get a chance." The gray snorted again, nodded his head fiercely as if agreeing, and then peered at Gib through his long, tangled forelock. Gib chuckled. Keeping his voice soft and low, he said, "Yep, I'm a-hearing you. And I bet I know a few more things about you. Somebody's been mighty mean to you lately. But you ought to be figuring it out that it wasn't me that did it. I never would take a whip to you or any other poor critter."

The talking went on for some time and after a while the big horse began to quiet down a little, but the rest of Gib's customers were getting noisier, nickering and whinnying and thumping impatiently on their stall doors. Demanding that Gib stop talking, they were, and start doing something about their empty mangers. It was while Gib was on the way to the loft that he figured out a way to solve the watering problem.

He fed and watered the rest of the horses first, stopping

101

in Silky's stall for just long enough to tell her she needn't be jealous of the newcomer.

"It's just that he's got a lot of problems that need to be taken care of in a big hurry," he told her as he set her water pail in the rack. "Once that's done, everything will be back to normal. And besides, he doesn't belong here like you do. Like as not we'll be sending him back to wherever he came from soon as this storm lets up, and things will be back the way they used to be 'tween you and me." But Silky still didn't seem too happy about it. She drank just a little bit and then pushed hard on Gib's shoulder with her wet nose, telling him she definitely didn't like having another horse taking up so much of his time. He gave her a last hurried pat and went on with his plan for taking care of the gray.

Gib started by picking one of the other empty stalls and fixing it up with fresh straw on the floor and a full water pail and manger. Then, leaving the door of that stall wide open, he headed back to the gray's. Moving quietly, Gib unlatched the stall door and then crouched down behind it as he pulled it slowly open. He was still hiding behind the open door when the big horse charged out past him and headed down the corridor at a gallop. At the closed barn door he skidded, reared, whirled around, and pounded back the other way. He passed the other stalls, where all four horses were looking out over their doors, trying to see what the commotion was about. But the gray only stopped once, long enough to sniff noses with Silky, before he charged on past where Gib was hiding and clear down to the other end of the barn.

When he came back he was moving more slowly, turning his head from side to side. Gib ducked his head and crouched lower. Unable now to see what was happening, he could only wait and listen, hoping to hear something that would let him know the gray's whereabouts. Time passed and Gib went on hiding, holding his breath and stretching his ears to listen. Silence. No sound at all except for a faint munching noise from the other end of the barn, where the other horses had gone back to their hay. At last Gib lifted his head very slowly and peeked out. A few feet away the gray was standing perfectly still just outside the newly stocked stall. Perfectly still except for his busy ears and eyes.

"Go on, boy. Go on in," Gib told him silently, behind clenched teeth. As if in answer the big horse finally moved forward into the stall and across it to the manger. He was busy with the oats when Gib closed the door, but as the latch slid into place with a thump the gray whirled and charged. The door held as the angry horse crashed into it, but the bared teeth just missed Gib's face as he ducked away.

The horse had gone back to his oats but Gib was still standing in the middle of the aisle, gulping and catching his breath when, at the other end of the barn, the main door creaked open.

"Gib," a whispery voice said, and there she was. Livy Thornton, bundled up like an Arctic explorer and frosted with snow, was standing in the wide open doorway.

Something, the shock perhaps of how close he'd come to having his face bit off, along with relief that his plan had worked, set off a kind of explosion somewhere in Gib's brain. Marching toward Livy, he began to tell her a thing or two in a tone of voice he didn't even know he had.

"Livy Thornton." The words sizzled like a boiling teakettle. "What in tarnation do you think you're doing? You could have gotten me killed, or gotten killed yourself. I just this minute got him shut up. If you'd come in half a second sooner he'd have trampled you flat as a pancake."

But Livy only stared at him, her expression going from shock to curiosity and then on to indignation. "Don't you yell at me, Gib Whittaker," she said. "I went to all the trouble to get bundled up like this and into these awful snowshoes just so I could help you out by taking care of the chickens, and all you can do is yell at me."

She whirled around then and started off through the snow, but after she'd gone a few steps, wide-legged and wobbly on the outsized snowshoes, she turned around and came right back.

"I want to see him. It want to see the ghost horse," she said. When Gib started to shake his head she added, "Why not? You said he was shut up now." Without waiting for an answer, she sidled around Gib and started down the aisle.

He caught up with her, grabbed her arm, and pulled her to a stop.

"All right," he whispered, "but stay back of me and be quiet."

At the gray's stall he pulled Livy to a stop, pushed her behind him, and tiptoed forward. The gray was at the manger eating hungrily, but he stopped long enough to snort and toss his head. Peering around Gib's shoulder, Livy gasped and then stared wide-eyed and openmouthed until he pulled her away.

Walking backward, still staring toward the gray's stall, Livy was babbling. "He's so big and beautiful," she said. "He's so—silvery, and the dapple spots are like snowflakes. Like snowflakes on silver." She stopped to look back again. "But what are those marks all over his back? Like something scratched him?"

As Gib opened the door he said, "Yeah, I guess something scratched him. But you listen to me, Livy Thornton. Don't you ever come out here again unless I know you're coming. You hear me?"

As Livy listened her eyes squinted up and her lips tightened and tipped down at the corners. "And you listen to me, Gib Whittaker. You've got no right to tell *me* what to do. And you know why."

Gib knew why, all right.

Chapter 15

On the third day of the storm it was still snowing, and the telephone wires were still down. Out in the barn the big gray horse went on being as wild and threatening as ever, and inside the Rocking M ranch house, the people around the kitchen table were tense and nervous. They were all anxious, first of all about Hy, who was still very sick, but also about Gib and the dapple gray.

Ever since that first morning when Gib was so late for breakfast the ladies had done a lot of fussing about the mysterious visitor. Fussing and insisting, at least Miss Hooper had, that she must see the animal that was taking up so much of Gib's time. Gib had thought up a lot of good excuses, the best one being that it was snowing too hard.

But that morning the sky cleared a bit and right after breakfast Miss Hooper announced that she was going to bundle up and go out to the barn to see the mysterious creature for herself. When Gib realized that Miss Hooper had made up her mind, he felt pretty frantic. Actually the horrible welts that crisscrossed the gray's body had gone down a bit already, and most of the bloody scabs had disappeared. In just a few more days the marks would hardly be noticeable, but they weren't there yet. Miss Hooper's sharp eyes were sure to spot them, and then she'd surely tell Missus Julia that the poor tortured animal in the barn would always be crazy with fear and anger.

Gib knew there was no stopping Miss Hooper when she got that look in her eyes, so he gave up and agreed. "Just let me go out first and pack the path down a little with my snowshoes," he insisted, and Miss Hooper agreed to that much of a postponement. That much, but no more. But those few extra minutes just might be enough for the plan Gib was working on. He was heading for the storm porch when, to his surprise, Livy said, "Me too. Wait a minute, Gib. I want to help pack the snow."

What made Livy's announcement especially surprising was that it was the first time she'd spoken to Gib since he'd ordered her out of the barn three days before. For a minute he thought his plan was ruined for sure, but then, remembering how long it always took Livy to get into her boots and snowshoes, he decided he still might have time to give it a try.

"All right, come on then," he told Livy. Then he broke every existing record getting into his barnyard gear, across the yard, and into the barn. Once there, he managed to get out of his snowshoes and climb up to unscrew the lightbulb nearest to the gray's stall, and then get back into his snowshoes and out the door before Livy came stomping across the yard.

The dim light was the first thing Miss Hooper remarked on when, bundled up to her eyeballs and galumphing along in a pair of men's wading boots, she made it out to the barn. "Awfully dim in here. What's wrong with the lights?" she said, and then, "And where is this mysterious animal of yours?" Gib was still pointing out the bulb and explaining that it must have just gone out, when they reached the gray's stall and the subject got changed in a hurry.

Even in the dim light the show the gray put on was pretty impressive. Obviously terrified of the unfamiliar people and voices, he pressed back against the far wall of his stall, snorting and pawing the earth, and now and then making threatening rushes toward the door.

Miss Hooper backed away, gasping loudly. "Good heavens," she said. "Dear me! Are you sure that door is strong enough to hold him, Gib? He seems completely wild."

Livy gasped too, but the things she was saying were quite different. What Livy was whispering was, "He's so beautiful. So fierce and beautiful." When it was over Gib thought it wasn't a very successful visit, but at least no one had mentioned the bullwhip scars.

Back in the kitchen there was a long discussion about

what should be done. Even after Gib explained how he'd worked out a safe way to feed and water the horse without getting near him, Miss Hooper kept saying that that wild animal should just be turned loose. "It's ridiculous," she said, "expecting Gib here to take care of that dangerous creature along with everything else he has to do. That horse came here from somewhere, and if he were turned loose he'd surely go back where he came from."

Gib shook his head. "He won't," he said. "He won't go back." But of course he couldn't say why. He couldn't say the poor horse would never go back to the place where he'd been beaten half to death. Not unless Gib wanted to risk being forbidden to go anywhere near the gray ever again.

But at last Missus Julia said, "I agree that it's a terrible responsibility for Gib. But the horse may not be able to go back to his owner, and if he doesn't he's quite likely to starve to death. Apparently he's not of prairie stock, and if he was stable raised he'd never make it on his own this time of year. Especially now when the snow is so deep."

Gib nodded hard. "That's right," he said. "He'd starve to death for sure. And he's not too much work for me. I've got lots of time now that we're not going in to school every day. And as soon as they get the phone lines up again we can find out who owns him, and they'll likely come to get him."

But Miss Hooper only snorted. "Hmmph," she said. "That is, if you manage to live that long."

Gib grinned. "You don't have to worry about that," he said. "I'm not going to take any chances. Besides, I think he's beginning to calm down a lot. Like as not he'll be gentle as a kitten in a few more days."

Miss Hooper humphed again and then Mrs. Perry, who'd been stoking up the fire in the kitchen range, got in on the conversation. Giving a big sigh, she said what a shame it was that Hy was sick, right now when he was needed so badly. "If Hy was only well enough to take care of things, or even to tell us what to do about Gib and that crazy animal, everything would be all right."

Everyone sighed and said, "Yes, yes, if only . . ." And, "Poor Hy. Poor, sick Hy." Even Livy had something to say. In a low voice so no one but Gib could hear she said, "Yes, and maybe when Hy is better I'll be able to go out to my own barn again without people yelling at me and telling me to stay away." Gib knew what she meant even though she didn't say what "people" she was talking about.

Maybe Gib had been exaggerating a little when he said the gray was beginning to calm down, but by the very next day it looked as how he'd actually been foretelling the future. There wasn't nearly as much snorting and threatening going on when he showed up that morning. And when Gib let the gray out he right off went looking for an open stall door instead of looking for somebody to attack.

"Hey there, boy, aren't you the smart one?" Gib told him. "Got it all figured out, haven't you? All you got to do is move to the next base like you were playing ball or something, and you win a clean stall and a big pan of oats."

Busy at the freshly stocked manger, the gray only rolled an eye in Gib's direction. His snort sounded more like a comment than a threat. Not a very polite comment maybe, but not too far from it.

That evening, after Gib spent the afternoon cleaning out all the other stalls, and an extra half hour grooming Silky, he still had to clean out the cowshed, milk Bessie, and take care of the chickens (Livy had quit helping with them) before he could go in and tell everybody the good news about the gray. But before he could even start telling his news he found out that Miss Hooper had some that was even better. Better and more important.

Hy was definitely on the mend. Miss Hooper said he'd finally passed the crisis and was feeling strong enough to start complaining again. "Says he's starving," she told Mrs. Perry. "Says he thinks we've been forgetting to feed him. And when I told him he'd been too sick to eat he said he'd never been that sick a day in his whole life."

Missus Julia said, "Thank God." Mrs. Perry said, "Glory be," and rushed off to the cellar for the makings for a big new pot of soup. And Gib felt a sudden lightening around his heart as if it was about to float up to the ceiling and take the rest of him along with it. An hour or so later when the soup was ready he asked to go with Miss Hooper when she took it up. But Miss Hooper said no, not yet.

"I know you, Gib Whittaker," she said. "I know you couldn't resist telling Hy about that wild horse of yours, and heavens knows you should, but not today. You know as well as I do that it would be just like that rascal to insist on getting up and going right out there to see for himself. So you just wait until tomorrow at least. All right?"

So Gib waited impatiently until the next day after dinner. Even then Miss Hooper made him promise not to stay too long and not to say anything that might worry Hy or encourage him to go out to see the dapple gray. "People who have had influenza often have relapses if they try to rush things," she said. "And I certainly don't want to put Hy, not to mention the rest of us, through any more of this sickbed routine."

So Gib promised, but it turned out to be not an easy promise to keep. The moment he started talking about the barn's new occupant, Hy's eyes went from sorry slits to wide and lively, and even his wrinkly skin seemed to take on a better color.

Hy wanted the complete story, which wasn't easy to do when there was so much that had to be left out. The horse Gib wound up describing was beautiful and hot-blooded, as well as wild and frightened, but that was all. Nothing at all about how fighting mad he was, or the horrible wounds that had made him that way.

Hy chuckled some when Gib told how he'd managed to clean the gray's stall and keep him fed and watered without ever going near him. "Right smart handlin'," he told Gib, "and you just be sure you go on handlin' him careful like. Don't go pushin' your luck with a wild one like that. Go on lettin' him keep his distance until . . ." He stopped then, and grinned for a moment. "But I'm forgettin' that you don't need anybody telling you how to speak horse lingo, Gib Whittaker. Figure you'll know what to do with that critter better than I can tell you."

Gib was pleased to hear Hy praise his horse handling, but he was disappointed that Hy didn't have any idea where the gray came from or who it might belong to. "Never did hear of any hot-blooded dapple gray in this neck of the woods," Hy said, shaking his head. "Somebody must have brought him in on the train in the last month or so, and judgin' by what you're telling me they must have paid a bundle for him."

And then beat him near to death, Gib wanted to say, but of course he didn't. Instead he went to look out the window at the snow. He was telling Hy how it had been snowing for so long he could hardly recollect what a clear day looked like, when Miss Hooper came in.

"Gibson," she said, "thought I told you to make it short. And as for you, Hyram Carter, you lie back now and relax, and stop even thinking about horses." Gib did what he was told and Hy appeared to be doing the same, except maybe for the not thinking about horses part, which Gib wouldn't have wanted to vouch for.

It was the very next day that the gray let Gib touch him for the first time. He came up to the stall door while Gib was talking to him and stretched out his neck until his nose just brushed Gib's hand before he snorted and shied away, back to the other side of the stall. And it was that same afternoon that Gib started bringing a pocketful of carrots with him whenever he showed up at the barn.

Gib found the carrots in the vegetable bin in the cellar and he was careful to take only the small wizened-up ones that Mrs. Perry wouldn't want to feed to humans. He knew Silky loved them and it turned out that the gray did too. And it was that same day that Gib started teaching him that he could have a carrot anytime he let himself be touched.

That evening after dinner Gib went up to talk to Hy again. They talked about the gray first and the other horses and then Hy brought up the weather. "It looks as how it's not fixin' to get any better soon," he said. "I seen a couple of winters like this afore, when the snow just kept a-comin' all winter long. Mighty hard on stock it is. And hard on any kind of wheeled contraption, like a wagon or buggy. If it goes on much longer you and me might have to ride into town and take the mules to pack in some provisions."

Gib said he could do that, but he didn't think it would be necessary anytime soon. "Mrs. Perry says she's got enough foodstuff in the cellar to feed us right through the winter."

"But how about school?" Hy asked. "Miss Hooper been keepin' you and Livy up to snuff on your lessons?"

Gib shook his head. "We haven't been doing much studying lately," he admitted. He decided against saying that both he and Miss Hooper had been too busy lately, what with all the extra doctoring and barnyard duties.

"It's a durn shame you and Livy are missin' out on so much schoolin' 'cause of a little bit of snow," Hy said. He shook his head. "And it's a double durn shame that Livy's pa never let her learn how to handle a horse. If she was half the horsewoman her mother was at her age, you and Livy could forget about that heavy old buggy and ride into school every day on Silky and Lightning."

That, Gib decided, was something to think about. To think about but not to mention to Livy. Not if he knew what was good for him.

Chapter 16

———◆◆◆———

Gib did know what was good for him, at least where Livy was concerned. So he certainly didn't mention what Hy had said about how they could have ridden Lightning and Silky to school, if Livy were half the horsewoman her mother had been. But it turned out that somebody else must have mentioned it. Either that or Livy had been listening outside Hy's door. Which, after all, was pretty likely. Livy had a special talent for that sort of thing.

The first hint Gib noticed was when Livy suddenly became more friendly, and a lot more helpful too. The very next morning she started taking care of the chickens again, and that same afternoon she asked Gib if she could come to the barn if she promised to knock before she came in and to do exactly what he told her to once she got inside. Gib was surprised.

"Well, I don't know," he said. "You'd have to ask your

mother about that I guess." And to his amazement she agreed to that too.

"You're right," she said. "I think I should ask her."

So when she showed up at the barn a couple of hours later he supposed that was what she'd done. He'd been in the barn for quite a while by then and most of his work was finished. The horses were all fed and the gray was safely shut in a freshened-up stall, when Gib heard the barn door rattling and somebody calling his name. It was Livy, all right, but this time, instead of barging on in, she opened the door just a crack and called to ask permission. Gib made one last check to be sure everything was secure before he told her to come ahead.

They went to look at the gray first and Gib showed Livy how much the ghost horse had quieted down. How he let Gib scratch his forehead now, and even pat his neck a little. Livy said again that he was the most beautiful horse in the world. And she also said, "I think it's just amazing how you've been able to calm him down so quickly."

Gib chuckled. "Nothing amazing about it," he said. "He's not mean. Just scared to death. I bet you'd act pretty mean too if you thought you were fighting for your life. But it didn't take him long to figure out that I wasn't fixing to hurt him. You're a smart one, aren't you, old boy?"

Gib was still talking to the gray and patting his neck when Livy sighed deeply. And when Gib just went on talking to the horse, she sighed more loudly. When he finally looked around she smiled and said, "I guess Hy's right about you after all, Gibson Whittaker."

"Right about me?" Gib asked cautiously. He'd known Livy long enough to know that when she used that tone of voice he needed to be on the lookout.

"Yes. When he said you had an absolutely magic touch with horses."

Gib grinned. "Hy said that?" he asked. But what he was thinking was that it didn't sound too likely. He knew that Hy thought he spoke "horse lingo," but an "absolutely magic touch" didn't sound a bit like anything Hy would say. What it sounded like, Gib thought, was that Livy was working up to something. And sure enough it turned out that she was. What Livy wanted was for Gib to give her riding lessons.

"Not on Silky," she said quickly. "I know I'm not ready for Silky. I learned my lesson about that. But maybe on Lightning? If you started in giving me lessons right away maybe I'd be able to start riding to school by the time Christmas vacation is over."

So that was the way it started. The very next day right after lunch Livy showed up in the barn wearing an old divided skirt and carrying a saddle. The skirt and the saddle, she told Gib, had been her mother's when she was a little girl, and they had been packed away in the bottom of an old trunk ever since. "Like she'd been saving them until I started riding," she told Gib, twirling around so he could get the whole picture. "Don't you think I look like a professional horsewoman?"

Gib had to agree that, sure enough, she looked like a horsewoman, before he headed down to the tack room for Lightning's bridle. Livy followed right behind him, chattering away about how she was probably going to be even more absolutely magical with horses than he was, because of being her mother's daughter, and a Merrill and all. She went on talking like that while she watched the saddling up. Then she followed Gib and Lightning to where a bench outside the tack room door made a handy mounting block.

But when Gib said, "All right. Up you go," she suddenly became very quiet. Pressed back against the wall, fists clenched and eyes wide, Livy stared at Lightning like she was scared to death. Like she was paralyzed with fear, actually, except that her lips were moving in an almost silent whisper.

"What?" Gib asked. "What are you saying?"

The whisper got a little louder. "I can't," Livy was saying. "I'm afraid."

"No, you're not." Gib grinned at her. "Remember, you weren't afraid before. When you got up on Silky you weren't afraid. Remember how—"

But Livy interrupted. Loudly. "I know," she said. "I wasn't afraid. And remember what happened. Remember how she bolted with me and—and—what happened to you, and everything."

119

Gib remembered. How Livy's getting ahead of herself and trying to ride Silky had almost gotten her thrown, and how Gib had been sent back to the orphanage because her father had blamed the whole thing on him.

It took a lot of talking on Gib's part, quiet talking about how Lightning wasn't Silky, and how they were going to take it easy and go real slow at first, before Livy climbed up on the mounting block and finally on up into the saddle. By the time Gib led Lightning up and down the aisle a couple of times she was herself again, talking and giggling and wanting to learn everything at once.

Lightning was very patient, walking up and down the corridor between the stalls and turning in circles over and over again without fretting or getting too frisky. Gib was surprised because, as Hy was always saying, Lightning had a full head of steam for an old codger, and he could be a mite headstrong at times, particularly when he hadn't been ridden regular. But now it was as if the old horse realized who was riding him and was taking the responsibility seriously. Gib was pleased with the old cow pony's performance and after they were through with the lesson he told him so while he gave him some extra oats and a good grooming.

Livy learned a lot that first day, things about using the reins and keeping your weight in your feet. And as it turned out, Gib learned a lot too. First of all he learned that Livy really had eavesdropped on his conversation with Hy. And, more importantly, that she hadn't asked her mother's permission to have a riding lesson. He hadn't been too surprised when Livy spilled the beans about the eavesdropping, because he already figured she'd done that. But when she made her other confession, on their way back to the house, it did put his back up a little.

"Livy Thornton," he was beginning when Livy interrupted to say, "I know. It was very sinful of me." She was hanging her head and looking pitiful as anything. After a minute she went on, "I *am* going to ask, though. I am going to get permission right away. Right now. As soon as we're back in the house." And when Gib gave her a look that said he didn't know whether to believe her or not she added, "You can come with me while I do it. And you can help me do it too. You can tell my mother how well I'm doing and what a good horsewoman I'm going to be. If you do, I'm sure she's going to say it's all right. My mother has always wanted me to ride, and besides, she thinks you're absolutely magical with horses."

Gib couldn't help grinning. Seemed as how a whole lot of people had been talking about how "absolutely magical" Gib Whittaker was.

They found Missus Julia in the library. She was reading a book and looking as filmy and elegant as always. Maybe almost too filmy, Gib thought, with her pale skin and those sorrowful shadows under her eyes. When she looked up and saw Gib and Livy the shadows faded, but then suddenly her welcoming smile changed to a questioning frown.

"Livy," she said, "is that my old riding skirt?" She didn't ask why Livy was wearing it, but the way she said it asked for her. And when Livy started to tell about the riding lesson the frown deepened.

"Livy Thornton," Missus Julia said, "I told you to stay away from that barn and you said you would. Gib has enough to handle out there without you complicating things. I can't believe you would—"

But Livy interrupted then by kneeling down by the wheelchair and putting her head in her mother's lap. She stayed there for a long time and for a while her mother only looked away while the sorrowful shadows returned to her face. At last Missus Julia sighed and asked, "What have the two of you been doing? Tell me about it, Gib."

Gib was still squirming and clearing his throat when Livy said, "It wasn't Gib's fault. It was Hy who said it would be a long time before anybody could get into Longford in a buggy. And Hy said it was a shame I didn't know how to ride because if I did Gib and I could ride Silky and Lightning to school." Livy raised her head then and looked at her mother. "I heard Hy say that, Mama. And Gib thought I had permission to learn. I didn't lie to him exactly but I made him think you'd said it was all right." She stopped talking then long enough to make a kind of sobbing sound before she went on, "I'm so sorry, Mama."

Livy really did look sorry but Missus Julia didn't seem to be accepting her apology, at least not right away. But then Livy sighed and, clasping her hands in front of her chest, said, "Oh, Mama, I just love horses now and I love riding too. And I'm learning really fast. Aren't I, Gib?"

So Gib said she was doing right well. But Missus Julia went on frowning until he added, "Comes by it natural, I guess. Having Merrill blood and all."

Missus Julia laughed then and said, "Gibson Whittaker. I declare, horses aren't the only creatures you know your way around." Then she sighed and said, "All right. I'll give you permission to go on with the lessons as soon as Hy is well enough to be there to keep an eye on—"

"But Mama," Livy interrupted. "We've already missed so much school. And if I have to wait until Hy is well we'll have to miss a lot more."

She went on arguing then about how careful they'd be and how calm and gentle Lightning was. At last Missus Julia sighed and said, "All right, all right. You may continue the lessons, Gib, as long as . . ." She turned toward Livy. "As long as you both promise to use Lightning. Lightning only. Not Silky. And Livy, you stay away, a long way away, from that dapple gray." She shook her finger. "You hear me, young lady?"

"Oh yes, I promise," Livy said. "I promise I won't even get near his stall. And Mama, I'm so happy that I'm finally going to learn how to ride, and I know you are too."

Livy left then to get cleaned up for supper, but as Gib started to go Missus Julia asked him to wait. "Don't go, Gib." She patted the sofa beside her chair. "Sit down a minute. I want to talk to you."

Gib sat, expecting more about Livy's riding lessons, but when Missus Julia started to talk it was about a different subject entirely. A subject that Gib had been wanting to bring up for a long time without knowing how to go about it. "Gib." Missus Julia looked almost as uncertain as Gib was beginning to feel. "Hy tells me that you've been concerned about"—she paused and smiled uneasily—"about, as Hy put it, 'having paperwork that says you belong to be here.' Is that right, Gib? Are you worried about that?"

Gib swallowed hard, shook his head, and nodded it almost at the same time. "Well, I was just wondering . . . ," he was starting to say when Missus Julia went on, "I want you to know that I wrote to Lovell House way back last November offering to sign adoption papers, but no one answered for a long time. I didn't write again as I probably should have because . . . Well, there were the blizzards and, as you know, I haven't been feeling very well. But just last week I finally did hear from Miss Offenbacher. Unfortunately, all she had to say was that you would have to come back and establish residency at Lovell House first, because Miss Hooper didn't fill out the proper forms before she took you away."

Gib was horrified and it must have showed because Missus Julia reached out and took both his hands in hers. "Don't worry, Gib," she said. "You won't have to go back. I've about decided that we'll just forget about the adoption effort. We'll let that Offenbacher woman go on biting off her own nose to spite her face. After all, a formal adoption isn't necessary to say that you are where you belong and you will stay here until . . ."

Gib looked up quickly as the old farm-out rule flashed through his mind. The rule about how a farm-out should be kept till he was eighteen and then paid fifty dollars and sent on his way. As if she had read his mind, Missus Julia shook her head slowly, her eyes softening toward tears. She pulled Gib toward her and touched his cheek as she went on, ". . . you'll stay here as long as ever you want to," she said softly. Then she turned him loose and told him to run along and not to worry anymore about adoption papers or anything at all. "Promise?" she said. "Promise me, Gib? No more worrying?"

So Gib promised, and he meant it too. After all, just like Missus Julia said—and Hy too—a piece of paper wasn't what made the difference. He wasn't going to think about it ever again.

After that the lessons continued. Every afternoon Gib saddled up Lightning, and Livy rode him up and down the corridor inside the barn. And after Livy's lesson was over and she'd gone back to the house Gib stayed on for a while. He groomed Lightning first off, and then did a little more teaching. But this time his student was the big gray, or Ghost, as Gib had started calling him.

Gib had to laugh a little, thinking about his two hard-headed students. The one that was likely to kick and bite, and the other one, which could be pretty dangerous too and a lot harder to predict. But they were both improving, there was no doubt about that. Livy had quit grabbing the saddle horn, and Ghost was letting Gib groom him a little without even threatening to bite. The whip marks were invisible now under his winter hair, but Gib could still trace them with his fingertips. They seemed to have reached the itchy stage, because Ghost obviously liked it when Gib scratched them gently with the currycomb.

The phone lines stayed down all that week, so the Rocking M continued to be completely cut off from human civilization, as Miss Hooper put it. At least until Wednesday, when Dr. Whelan showed up plowing through snowdrifts on his long-legged chestnut mare. He'd come, he said, to check on both his patients, Mrs. Thornton and Hy as well. Folks in Longford had been worried about them, Doc Whelan said, and he was right glad that he could go back and put their minds at rest.

But the doctor didn't put Gib's mind to rest any about Ghost. When Gib asked the doc if he'd heard anything about a dapple gray that had gone missing he said he hadn't, but he'd let Gib know if he did. And he also said that

Hy wasn't to even think about going outside anytime soon, and that they all should be very careful not to say anything that would make him think he had to. Like telling him about any kind of barnyard problems that needed his immediate attention.

"And we shouldn't tell him about the riding lessons either," Missus Julia told Gib and Livy later. "Because he'd be bound to think it was his duty to be out there keeping an eye on things."

By the day before Christmas the snow had firmed up some and, for the first time, Livy's riding lesson moved out to the big corral. Gib went out first on Silky and let her work the kinks out and, at the same time, pack the snow down a little, before he went back to the barn for Livy on Lightning. Then the two of them rode around the corral side by side.

They started trotting lessons that day and Livy kept asking Gib to tell her how to ride out the trot the way he did. "With-out-boun-cing-like-this," she said with a bounce between every syllable. It wasn't, Gib discovered, an easy thing to explain and no matter what he told her she went right on bouncing. But when he said he thought they'd had enough practice for one day, she didn't want to stop. Gib told her she might be sorry tomorrow, but she only shrugged and said, "Don't be silly. I feel fine." But the next day Gib noticed her walking kind of stiff-legged, and for the first time she suggested they should take a day off.

"After all, it is Christmas," she said, "and nobody should have lessons on Christmas day. Not even riding lessons."

Christmas was different that year, that was for sure. No dinner party for Longford guests and not even any fancy decorations. But Mrs. Perry cooked a special dinner with ham and sweet potatoes, and Hy made it extra special by coming to the table for the first time since the influenza. And there were gifts too, some of them handmade, and a few from the Sears, Roebuck catalog.

Gib got a new jacket, which Miss Hooper had cut down from one that had been Mr. Thornton's, and two pairs of hand-knitted socks. Gib didn't have much to give. He surely would have liked to have had something better for the ladies than the letter openers he'd carved from an old chair leg he'd found in the basement. And for Hy a hand-made frame for a Will James drawing of a bucking horse that Hy had cut out of a magazine and tacked up on his wall. But with no way to get into town, and no money to spend if he'd gotten there, it was the best he could do.

The day after Christmas the lessons in the big corral started up again, and the other secret ones with the Gray Ghost went on too.

Chapter 17

Ghost wasn't a mean-natured horse any more than Silky was. He was just scared and angry and, Gib found out, definitely head-shy. Even after he'd started being real welcoming when Gib showed up with a currycomb and a pocketful of carrots, he didn't like having his head touched. At least not by a hand that had anything in it. Right at first he even shied away from a brush if it got too near his head. And the first time Gib tried to put a halter on him things got pretty lively for a while.

When Gib came in carrying the halter Ghost took one look and turned back into the wild-eyed thing he'd been when he first showed up, snorting and rearing and threatening to bite. It took a lot of slow, easy talk and a carrot or two before he would even come close enough to get a good look at the halter. But after he'd shoved it around with his nose he seemed to calm down some, and before long Gib was able to slip it on his head. And when Gib clipped on a lead rope the big gray let himself be led up and down the barn corridor with no fuss at all, except for a few snorts and nickers at the other horses as he passed their stalls. And when Gib brought in a saddle and blanket, things went even more smoothly.

But the next step was the bridle and that was when Gib began to find out where the trouble lay. There was, Ghost told Gib plain as day, no way in the world he was going to let that bit be put in his mouth. And even after Gib reasoned with him for a long time he didn't look to be changing his mind one little bit.

That night Gib did a lot of thinking about Ghost's problem. So much thinking, in fact, that he was kind of absentminded at the dinner table. The rest of them happened to be talking about earthquakes and tornados, but Gib kept forgetting to listen to what was being said. And of course he couldn't mention what he was thinking about because they'd all promised not to mention any urgent barnyard problems around Hy.

"And where do you suppose our Mr. Whittaker is tonight?" Miss Hooper wanted to know. "Certainly not here with the rest of us. Haven't heard two words out of him since we sat down."

"That's for sure," Hy said. "I been noticin' that too. What you been mullin' over so hard, pardner?"

Gib laughed and said he guessed he'd been woolgathering, all right. "I was listening, though. I heard what everybody was saying about that earthquake in California."

They all laughed then and Livy said, "That was at least half an hour ago. Just now we were talking about President Taft and before that it was coyotes. Where have you been, Gib?"

When Gib said he didn't know, Livy said, "Well, I do. Out in the barn trying to get that wild . . . Oops."

There were frowns all around the table and Livy must have gotten the message because she swallowed the rest of what she was saying with a big forkful of mashed potatoes, and the conversation went back to politics and President Taft. Gib made an effort to get back into the discussion but without much luck.

When the meal was over Gib didn't stay downstairs to read or play games the way he sometimes did. After he'd helped Hy up the stairs he went on to his own room. What he was tempted to do was to go back to Hy's room and just plain out ask him what he thought was the matter with a horse that didn't even hump his back when you saddled him, but who went crazy when you tried to make him take a bit. But he knew that was exactly the kind of thing you didn't want to mention to Hy Carter. Not unless you wanted him to be on his way to the barn immediately, influenza or no influenza.

So no good advice from Hy. But later that night while Gib was waiting to go to sleep he began to develop a theory of his own. He was still making plans for testing it out when he finally fell asleep, and went right on solving head-shy horse problems in his dreams.

But the next day was Thursday and, with the end of Christmas vacation only a few days away, Livy insisted that she needed a special riding lesson. A lesson that would include some time outside on the open road. Which, Gib had to admit, made a certain amount of sense. Riding down the snowy driveway and then out onto the Longford road was likely to present some problems that you wouldn't run into trotting around inside a corral. So after they'd been around the corral a few times Gib unlatched the gate and off they went down the Rocking M's long drive.

There'd been a couple of inches of fresh snow the night before, but now the sky was a clear, cold blue. Under the thin layer of fluffy stuff, the remains of the old snowpack were still unthawed, so the footing was pretty tricky. Old Lightning, who'd probably seen lots of bad weather in his time, took it calm and easy, and even Silky, after a few snorting, plunging protests, settled down to businesslike behavior. On the driveway some of the drifts were almost up to the horses' bellies and as they struggled forward, their heavy breathing sent twin plumes of frozen mist from their distended nostrils.

Right at first Livy's face had been tight with fear, but halfway down the drive she began to relax. "Look at the horses' breath," she said. "They look like smoke-breathing dragons." She giggled. "I was scared at first but I like it now. Do you suppose we could go all the way to Longford today? It ought to be easier once we get out on the main road where the snow's been packed down a little."

But Gib, who was anxious to get back to the barn to try out his theory about Ghost, said he didn't think they should go too far on the first day. "Got to break the horses in to heavy going like this kind of gradual-like," he argued, and after a while Livy agreed.

"All right," she said, "let's turn around. Right now. I think Lightning is getting tired, and besides my nose is freezing."

Back in the barn with Lightning and Silky taken care of, and with Livy off to the house to warm up her nose, Gib went looking for a hackamore he remembered seeing somewhere in the tack room. Sure enough, there it was on a high peg under a bunch of old broken halters. It was a nice one. Made mostly of horsehair rope, it had a leather chin strap, but the knot that went under the chin was a large ball of braided rope. Gib examined it carefully. He'd never used a hackamore instead of a bridle before, but he knew how it was supposed to work. The reins were attached so that when you pulled on them the knot pressed under the horse's chin and the pressure told him to stop. In general, what Gib had heard was that you didn't have

nearly as much control as you did with a bit, so hackamores were usually used only on a mount that was pretty
easy to control.

"Well," Gib told Ghost as he walked into the stall carrying the hackamore. "Can't say as how you're all that gentle,
pardner, but what I think is that somebody's really turned
you against having a rough old iron bit in that soft mouth of
yours. So lets see how you're going to take to this contraption."

Like before, the saddling went without a hitch, but when
Gib started to slip the hackamore over the gray's nose
there was some pretty suspicious snorting and head tossing. But Gib made a lot of soft talk, telling Ghost, "See,
there's no bit here. Just like another halter, is all it is. Nice
soft halter with nothing that has to go inside your mouth."

A lot of such soft talk and a few carrots later, Gib led
Ghost out into the corridor wearing a cinched-up saddle
and, on his head, an old braided horsehair hackamore. Using the reins as a lead rope, Gib led Ghost up and down the
aisle a few times before he pulled him to a stop.

Talking all the time, he lined the gray up, adjusted the
reins, and started to ease himself up into the saddle. But
Ghost didn't like it. His ears flicked backward and he side-
stepped before Gib could get his foot clear into the stirrup.
But after some more soft talk and a couple more circles up
and down the aisle, Gib tried again. And this time Ghost

stayed put, even when Gib put his foot in the stirrup, put some weight on it, waited a moment, and then swung up into the saddle.

"Okay, boy," Gib said as he touched his heels to the gray's flanks. "Here we go."

The big horse's head went up. He snorted softly and began a dancing, head-tossing movement down the corridor. They were almost to the barn door when, holding his breath, Gib leaned the reins to the left across the powerful gray neck. Immediately Ghost turned left in a sharp circle. Letting his breath go in a puff of relief, Gib grinned. Just as he'd figured, Ghost certainly had been trained to neck rein. There was no problem there.

But the important test came at the other end of the corridor when Gib pulled back on the reins and whispered, "Whoa." The gray hesitated, tossed his head anxiously, and then, responding to the pressure on the noseband and the lump of rope under his chin, came to a stop. Grinning again, Gib patted the gray's neck, telling him over and over again what a good boy he was and how well he was doing. And he was too, letting a pull on the reins tell him to stop even though there was no controlling bit in his mouth.

It had gone so well that Gib didn't want to stop, but it was getting late and there were still the chores to be done. Tomorrow, he told Ghost, they'd be branching out. Going out into the outside world. "Yes, sir," he said as he pulled off the saddle and led the gray into his stall. "Tomorrow's going to be the big day. Tomorrow we're going to see what you can do outside this old barn. Out there in the big old scary world."

Chapter 18

Gib hadn't thought it would be an easy day, and it wasn't. After the usual barnyard chores, there was saddling up Lightning and Silky for Livy's riding lesson, which turned out to be a long one, followed by a rubdown for both horses. It wasn't until midafternoon that Gib was able to keep his promise to Ghost.

The saddling up went without a hitch, but the moment Gib started to lead him across the barnyard Ghost became a different animal. A head-tossing prancer, whose sideways skittering almost jerked Gib off his feet two or three times before they reached the corral. And once inside the gate it took a lot of soft talk and several tries before Ghost would let Gib get close enough to swing up into the saddle.

Sitting on Ghost for the first few turns around the corral was something like riding on a barrel of dynamite. A barrel that threatened to explode at any minute. He didn't buck, at least not exactly, but he surely wasn't paying much heed to what Gib was telling him to do. Plunging forward, dancing sideways, rearing and tossing his head, he rounded the corral at least a half dozen times before he settled enough to respond to the reins, and to the sound of Gib's voice telling him, "Take it easy. Settle down now, you high-stepping rascal." But when he did start listening a little Gib put him to working out his nervous energy by rounding and rerounding the corral, crossing and crisscrossing it in sharp figure eights.

The figure eights were high-legged and sideways at first. It wasn't until a half hour or so had passed that they settled into a steadier trot, and finally an almost flat-footed, down-to-earth walk. Gib knew that one reason for the better behavior was that the gray was getting tired, but there was more to it than that. It seemed to Gib that Ghost was settling down because he was beginning to figure out that he wasn't about to be hurt. Wasn't about to be punished by bit and whip the way he'd surely been before.

By the time Gib took him back to the barn the sweated-up, hard-breathing gray was listening again, not only to the reins but also to the sound of Gib's voice telling him what a great job he'd done.

Gib was mighty tired that night. Even after he'd cooled Ghost down and groomed him there were still the milking and the other evening chores to be taken care of. When dinner was over all Gib wanted to do was to go to his room and collapse, but Livy wanted him to stay downstairs and talk for a while. To talk, she said, about Monday, and their first ride to school.

"And something else," she whispered as soon as they were out of hearing of the adults. Her eyes flickered excitedly as she went on. "There's something else I want to tell you about too. Something secret." She glanced around the library to where her mother was reading a book and Miss Hooper was writing a letter. "We have to go somewhere we can talk without anyone listening."

She looked around the room for a moment longer before she said loudly, "I know. Let's play dominoes. Come on, Gib, I want to play dominoes."

Gib didn't feel a bit like playing dominoes, but he saw right away what Livy was setting up. The game table was way across the room in the bay window alcove, where it would be possible to talk without being overheard as long as they kept their voices down. So he let himself be led over to the alcove and helped get the tiles turned over and stirred around. As soon as she'd drawn her tiles Livy plunked down a double-four and then forgot all about the game. "I saw you," she whispered, leaning forward. "I was looking out of the window. Upstairs where you can see the corral. And I saw you riding the gray." Her eyes were glittering.

Gib chuckled, shaking his head. "He's pretty rambunctious, all right."

"Rambunctious?" Livy raised her eyebrows. "A lot worse than rambunctious. I really thought you were going to get killed right there in front of my eyes." She sighed shakily. "It was so exciting."

"That right?" Gib asked, straight-faced. "That must have been pretty exciting, all right. Not every day you get to see somebody getting killed."

Livy frowned. "That's not what I meant and you know it, Gib Whittaker. I just meant it was so—thrilling. Like watching them ride the bucking broncos at the Longford rodeo. Only even more thrilling because those bony old rodeo broncos aren't nearly as beautiful as Ghost is. He's so magnificent and—wild."

"No, not wild." Gib shook his head. "He's been stable-raised and trained too. Real well trained, I think. It's just that he was kind of crazy when he first got here."

"Crazy?" Livy was fascinated. She stared at Gib and he stared back, thinking how Livy's face with its big eyes and sharp-edged cheekbones had a way of putting him in mind of a hot-blooded horse. A horse that was full of life and fire and—the thought made him grin—a lot of downright muleheadedness.

"Well, maybe not crazy," he said. "But awful scared. Somebody's scared him real bad and hurt him too."

"Hurt him?" Livy's eyes were wide and demanding. "How do you know? Tell me."

All right, he thought. I guess you ought to know. So he

told her about the whip marks. Not making it as bad as it really was, but enough to make her understand how serious the problem had been. "He was scared, but he was angry too," Gib said. "Mighty angry and looking to get even."

Livy was glaring now. "That's terrible," she said. "How could anybody do a thing like that? Whoever it was ought to be shot. He ought to be tied up and—" Suddenly she stopped raving and told Gib to get busy and play. "They're watching us," she said. "Hoop is. Go on, play a tile."

So Gib put down a four-two, and they went on playing until the game was finished and Livy had won. Actually Gib helped her just a little because he knew she'd never quit until she'd won, and right at that moment he was mostly interested in getting up to bed. Livy didn't say any more about the gray until the game was over, but as they were putting away the tiles she whispered, "Are you going to ride him again tomorrow?" And when Gib said he was hoping to she said, "Good. Tell me when, because I want to watch again."

It was late Saturday afternoon, with the chores and Livy's riding lesson finally finished, before Gib had time to get the gray saddled up and ready for another ride in the corral. Late in the afternoon on a darkening day with such a heavy mist in the air that halfway across the barnyard everything faded into blurry shadows. The weather, Gib thought, was playing the same sorts of tricks as it had that morning when Ghost had first appeared at the Rocking M. An icy fog had come in, like the one out of which a huge silvery shadow of a horse had appeared and then, just as swiftly, faded away.

Looking around the mist-shrouded barnyard, Gib couldn't help shivering, even though he was warmly dressed. There was something mysterious about the blinding fog. Mysterious and cold too. Terribly cold and getting colder by the minute. As he led Ghost across the barnyard Gib told him it was going to be a short lesson. "So you'd better concentrate on learning something in a hurry, before we both freeze solid," he told the prancing gray. And Ghost, throwing his head violently up and down, seemed to be saying that he wanted to hurry too. "All right, all right," he seemed to be telling Gib. "Stop talking and let's get started."

Ghost started out pretty lively again. Plunging and sidestepping and tossing his head, he managed to keep Gib too busy to notice much of anything besides the dapple gray powder keg he was sitting on. It did occur to him, after a while, to wonder if Livy was watching from the upstairs window, like she'd said she was going to. But when he looked up toward the house the drifting mist made it impossible to tell whether anyone was there or not. Gib forgot about being watched then and concentrated on getting Ghost to stop the nonsense and quiet down.

It was Ghost who saw them first. Something near the gate spooked him into a sideways sashay so sudden that it almost left Gib behind. It wasn't until he'd regained his balance and got the gray to quit acting the fool that he saw what the trouble was. Right outside the gate a tall man wearing a big Stetson and woolly chaps was sitting on a Roman-nosed buckskin. Gib recognized the horse first, and then the man. Yes, it surely was the Thorntons' neighbor, Mr. Clark Morrison.

Gib was reining Ghost back toward the gate and fixing to call howdy, when Morrison started shouting. "My God, boy," was what he yelled. "Get off that horse before you get killed."

Chapter 19

———————

In the first few seconds after Mr. Morrison appeared at the corral gate, Gib was too busy quieting the gray to think about what the man had yelled, and what it might mean. But by the time Ghost's plunging dash toward the other end of the corral had finished up in a skittering sideways dance, the questions had begun to shape themselves inside his head.

Why did Mr. Morrison yell at Gib to get down before he got killed? Did he know something about Ghost? And if he did, why did he? Was it because—the thought hit Gib like a kick in the stomach. Was it because Ghost belonged to him? And if he did, did that mean that he was the one who . . . ?

As Gib dismounted and led the fretting, head-tossing horse to the gate, the rest of that question was churning around inside his head and threatening to spill out of his

144

mouth in an angry yell. But Morrison was no longer in asking distance. He had ridden off to the other side of the barnyard, and there he sat on his big buckskin, watching and waiting while Gib led Ghost back toward the barn. Gib blinked hard and shook his head, trying to see Morrison through a vivid memory of scabbed and bloodstained ridges on dapple gray flanks. Clenching his teeth, he looked back to where Morrison was following along behind, leading the buckskin. But when Gib slowed down to let him catch up Morrison slowed too. At the barn door he stopped altogether and waited until Gib unsaddled Ghost and put him in his stall. It was only then that Morrison came on into the barn and began to ask questions. To ask, but not to answer any, at least not right at first.

Morrison had lots of questions. "All right, young man, what are you doing with my horse? Who told you you could ride him? Did Carter let you do that? I can't believe Hyram Carter would be fool enough let a boy ride a dangerous animal like that."

Swallowing down some questions of his own, questions about horse beaters and bullwhips, Gib managed to squeeze out an answer to Morrison's question about Hy. Between clenched teeth he said, "Hy has nothing to do with this, Mr. Morrison. He's been sick in bed for almost a month. Real bad influenza."

Morrison frowned. His voice had a tight, angry sound as he asked, "Do you mean to tell me Carter doesn't know that he has an extra horse in this barn? A horse that just happens to be a valuable Kentucky Thoroughbred? And how about Mrs. Thornton? She doesn't know either?"

Gib found himself explaining that yes, she knew he was there, all right. "But she doesn't know where he came from or who he belongs to. Nobody does. Mrs. Thornton tried to call the livery stable to ask if they knew where he came from, but our phone line was down. We asked Doc Whelan too, when he came to see to Hy, but he hadn't heard of anybody losing a dapple gray."

Mr. Morrison seemed to calm down a little then, and when Gib started explaining how the gray had appeared outside the barn in the middle of the snowstorm, he finally began to really listen. "He was in bad shape." The sharp edge of anger was back in Gib's voice, and probably in his eyes too, as he repeated, "Real bad shape."

"Bad shape?" Morrison's eyes narrowed suddenly and he reached out and took hold of Gib's shoulder. "How do you mean, bad shape?"

Gib pulled away. He tried to swallow the anger down but it was still there in his voice as he said, "Well, he was ganted up pretty bad, ribs showing and all." He turned his back then and, gathering up the tack, headed down the corridor, trying to get away and calm down long enough to decide how much else to say, and how to say it. To decide whether to tell the man who'd probably done it about the bloody welts that crisscrossed Ghost's barrel and flanks.

But Morrison followed him and went right on asking questions all the way to the tack room door.

One of the questions he asked was what the date had been when the gray appeared at the Rocking M. Gib wasn't sure of the day exactly, but he did remember it was on the second day of the big snowstorm.

"The day after the storm started." Mr. Morrison was nodding slowly. "That means—that means—"

Gib interrupted. "Don't you know when he ran away?"

Morrison shrugged impatiently. "No. No I don't. Not exactly. I was in Chicago for almost a month. Just got back a few days ago."

Gib stared in surprise and disbelief and then, as he began to understand, with a feeling of relief so strong that it almost made him smile. Relief that maybe it hadn't been Morrison after all who had beaten Ghost. It hadn't been the man who owned him and would surely take him back and own him again. As he turned away to lift his saddle up on the rack Gib must have sighed out loud. "What is it, boy?" Morrison asked sharply. "What aren't you telling me?"

It came pouring out then like a river breaking over a dam. "He'd been beaten, real bad," Gib said. "With a bullwhip or something that cut right through the hide. There were big welts all over him. Bloody ones." He motioned toward the gray's stall. "They're better now. The scabs are all off, but you can still feel some scars there under the hair when you run your fingers over his flanks."

"Beaten? With a bullwhip?" Morrison was staring at Gib. Staring and shaking his head and still muttering under his breath as he started up the corridor toward the gray's stall. When Gib caught up with him Morrison was standing at the stall door, staring at Ghost with a kind of twitching around his eyes and mouth that almost looked like he was fixing to yell, or else to cry.

"See there on his flank," Gib said. "You can still see one of the worst places, and you can still feel a lot of them."

"Yes, yes, I see it." Morrison's voice quavered a little. "Rafe said he thought that miserable charlatan beat him, but I had no idea he used a bullwhip."

"Charlatan?" Gib said.

"A fake, and a liar. Named Dettner. Lou Dettner." The name came with a sizzle as if Morrison had squeezed it out between his teeth. "Claimed he was one of the best horse wranglers in the Midwest. I left him in charge of the riding stock when I went away, and when I came back the gray was missing and so was Dettner. Rafe said Dettner whipped the horse until he broke free and ran. Ran right over him, Rafe said. Knocked him down and maybe broke his arm. Then Dettner packed up and left the ranch." Morrison looked at Gib sharply. "You heard of a trainer named Dettner?" he asked.

Gib shook his head. "Don't know of anyone by that name. But Hy might. Hy knows just about every wrangler and broncobuster in the country. I've heard him say so lots of times."

"Hmm," Morrison said. "I'll bet he does." He nodded once or twice more before he went on. "I surely would like to talk to your Mr. Carter, that is if he's up to it. What do you think, boy? Is Hy well enough to have a visitor for a few minutes?"

So Gib said he thought Hy might be well enough, but that he'd have to ask Miss Hooper. "Up till yesterday," Gib said, "she wouldn't let me tell him anything that might start him to fretting. Hy knows about the gray being here, but I didn't tell him about the whip marks or about how . . ." Gib stopped to consider how to put it. "Or even about how wild-acting he was, at least right at first. I didn't tell Hy anything about that. He's a lot better now, but you better ask first."

Mr. Morrison said he understood about Hy's illness, and that he wouldn't even go near Hy until he'd talked to Miss Hooper. "I've met your Miss Hooper," he said, "and I quite agree that one would do well to get her permission first. So . . ." He put his hand on Gib's shoulder. "That's what we'll do, Gibson, if you'll lead the way. We'll get permission from Miss Hooper and then we'll see what Mr. Hyram Carter can tell us."

As they started for the barn door Morrison stopped at Silky's stall, so Gib did too. And of course Silky came to see him, nickering and nudging Gib with her soft nose. Watching Silky, Morrison shook his head regretfully. "There's the beautiful lady who got me into this whole mess," he said. And when Gib stared at him in confusion he went on to explain. "Lit a fire in my belly, she did. A feeling I just had to own something even halfway that magnificent." As Morrison reached out to pat Silky's nose she flicked her ears back and pulled away, but she didn't try to bite.

"After I saw her that day," Morrison went on, "I just couldn't get her out of my mind. But I found out soon enough that Mrs. Thornton wasn't at all interested in selling. Then just a day or two later while I was still all fired up about owning a Thoroughbred, I heard from a friend of mine who was about to leave for Kentucky on a horse-buying trip."

They left the barn then and, as they crossed the barn-yard, Morrison went on with his story. "I asked this friend who was supposedly an authority on hot-blooded horses to pick one out for me. Not necessarily with a great track record, I told him. I didn't care about that. But I wanted something from a good bloodline. Didn't even care if it was a mare or gelding, as long as it was good-looking and well trained. That's what I especially asked for," he said in a sarcastic tone of voice. "Well trained." He rolled his eyes and nodded back toward the barn. "And he came back with that dapple gray devil."

Gib shook his head, wanting to say that Ghost was no

devil. Just a poor scared-to-death critter who thought he was fighting for his life. But Morrison was still talking. "Right at first, the day I saw him coming down out of that boxcar, I thought I'd gotten my money's worth and then some. Beautiful thing to look at, isn't he?"

Gib agreed. "Yes," he said. "Yes, sir. Mighty good-looking."

Morrison shook his head as he went on, "Good to look at, all right. But I'm afraid old Famous Fox isn't good for much else. Been nothing but trouble for me from the moment he got here."

"Famous Fox?" Gib asked.

Morrison nodded. "Pedigree name. Comes from a great bloodline, he does." He sighed. "But as far as I'm concerned he's been a real nightmare." He grinned ruefully. "Threw me off the first time I rode him. Broke three ribs and nearly broke my wrist."

"He bucked?" Gib was asking as he led the way into the storm porch. "He's never bucked with—"

But just at that moment the door that led to the kitchen flew open. Flew open and slammed back against the wall, and there Livy stood with her hands on her hips, blocking the entrance to the kitchen.

"Gib," she started to say, "what on earth . . . ?" She stopped then, staring at Mr. Morrison. "What are you doing here?" she demanded.

Chapter 20

Morrison looked startled. "Well, hello there, young lady," he said. "I was just dropping by to see how you folks were getting along, but I can see that I should have been here a whole lot sooner. Seems you folks have been putting up with my rascal of a runaway horse." He stopped then, smiling at Livy uneasily. Gib didn't wonder. The look on Livy's face was enough to make anyone feel uneasy.

"Your horse?" she asked, and then, "Oooh. You mean Ghost? You mean Ghost is yours?"

"Ghost?"

"That's what we've been calling him," Gib explained. "Gray Ghost, or just plain Ghost."

"Oh, I see," Mr. Morrison said. "Yes, he's mine, all right. But he's been missing for almost a month. Couldn't believe my eyes when I rode in here and saw him out there in the corral." He turned to hang up his coat. Turned his back on where Livy was staring at him with her eyes getting flatter and meaner every second.

Watching her, Gib saw that her whole face—tight lips, angry cat eyes, and jutting chin—was warning that some kind of an explosion was about to happen. And from past experience he was pretty sure that everyone would be better off if he could pull the fuse. Grabbing her arm, Gib whispered in her ear, "He couldn't have done it, Livy. He was in Chicago. It was somebody else who whipped Ghost."

It took a minute for Gib's message to sink in. When it did, Livy's storm-cloud face cleared a little. Not all the way, but enough to make Gib think she might be willing to hear a little more before she started screeching. But she obviously wasn't entirely convinced.

"All right," she whispered to Gib. "Then who did it? And what are you going to do about it?"

"That's what we're going to find out," Gib told her. "Soon as you get out of the way and let us in the house."

Reluctantly Livy backed up, and when Gib asked she said her mother wasn't feeling well and couldn't be bothered, but that Miss Hooper might be around somewhere. Gib found Miss Hooper easily enough, writing in an account book at the library desk. But when he told her what the situation was and asked her if Mr. Morrison could talk to Hy she shook her head. And went on shaking it while Gib told her that the dapple gray runaway belonged to Morrison.

"So he was the one who turned him into an outlaw. Somehow I'm not surprised to hear that," she said.

So Gib hurried to explain again about how Mr. Morrison had been in Chicago and a wrangler he'd hired had been the one who mistreated Ghost and made him run away. By the time Gib got to the part about Dettner, Miss Hooper was still shaking her head, but a little more slowly. And when he said, "He just wants to find out if Hy knows anything about a man named Dettner. That's all," she finally gave a reluctant nod.

She got to her feet then and said she wanted to have a word with Mr. Morrison before she decided what ought to be done. They found Mr. Morrison and Livy still in the kitchen, standing on different sides of the room and watching each other nervously out of the corners of their eyes.

"Ah, Miss Hooper," Morrison said, looking mighty relieved. Gib couldn't help sympathizing, knowing from firsthand experience what that glare of Livy's could do to a body's peace of mind.

"It's so good to see you again," Morrison went on, bowing over Miss Hooper's hand. He looked pretty phony, Gib thought, and judging by her suspicious expression, Miss Hooper seemed to be feeling the same way. When Morrison said, "I'd really like to talk to Mr. Carter for a few minutes if you think he's up to it. Just want to ask a couple of questions about—" she nodded sharply.

"I know, I know," she interrupted impatiently. "Gib told me what it's about. Mr. Carter's health has improved, but just to be on the safe side I'd like to be present at this interview. To make sure my patient doesn't get too worked up." She looked at Gib then and her frown didn't disappear except a little around her eyes. "Hy gets worked up easily where horseflesh is concerned. Isn't that right, Gibson?"

As Gib was agreeing, Miss Hooper told him, "You come along too. Hy's been asking to see you." As the three of them started for the stairs, a fourth party was suddenly right behind them. "I'm coming too," Livy said, and she did.

At Hy's room Miss Hooper knocked, went in, and in a moment came back for the rest of them. Hy was sitting up in bed wearing a striped nightshirt and a surprised expression. But outside of the widening eyes and arched eyebrows, he looked pretty much like his old self. "Well, well," he said. "Would you look at that? What's this about?" The wrinkle gullies rearranged themselves into a grin as he went on, "Hope you folks aren't here to pay your last repects, 'cause I'm not fixing to kick the bucket anytime soon."

Everyone laughed, Morrison hardest of all. "Glad to hear it, Mr. Carter," he said. "Right pleased to hear that you're planning to be around for a while longer, because I really need your help. Need to ask for some information on a very important matter."

"Is that a fact?" Hy said. "Well, I never set myself up to be no fountain of wisdom, but I'd be right glad to be of help if I'm able."

So then Morrison started in telling how his old wrangler, Jim Peters, had gone off to Arizona when winter set in, and he'd had a hard time finding someone to take his place. "Then around the first of November, I met a fellow who claimed to be a first-class trainer and broncobuster. So I put him on the payroll right away because I had a long trip to Chicago coming up and I needed to have the edge taken off some raw broncs I'd just bought." He paused and grinned shamefacedly as he went on, "Not to mention a Thoroughbred I'd been fool enough to buy." He looked over at Gib as he went on, "A dapple gray that I take it you've been hearing something about, from Gibson here."

"Yeah." Hy's nod was slow and thoughtful. " 'Spect you're right about that. Gib's been telling me about a fancy gray that showed up here durin' the big snow." He paused, scratching his head. "So I take it it was this new hand of yours who let the gray get away?" And when Morrison opened his mouth to answer, Hy went on, "And what might this wrangler feller's name be?"

"Called himself Dettner," Morrison said. "Lou Dettner."

Hy let out a long whistle. "Dettner," he said. "I sure as the world thought that two-legged rattlesnake would have got himself lynched by now."

Hy went on then to tell one of his long-winded stories about this cowhand name of Dettner who had been kicked off nearly every ranch in four states because he had, as Hy put it, a mean streak wider than the Mississippi. "Not a bad hand in some ways," Hy said. "Could ride and rope with the best of them, but he didn't like to be crossed by man nor beast. Came near to killing a young cowhand he took a dislikin' to, not to mention what he did to a whole lot of livestock."

Hy's eyes suddenly lost their storytelling cloudiness and fastened on Morrison. "So what's Dettner up to now? Got anything to do with that dapple gray Gib's been riding herd on?"

Morrison took a breath and opened his mouth wide to start answering, before he glanced over at Miss Hooper and shut it again. After he'd thought for a moment he said carefully, "Well, he let the gray get away from him, for one thing, just as the blizzard was blowing in. That must have been when the horse showed up here."

But when Hy started to ask some more questions Miss Hooper said visiting time was over and shooed everyone out of the room. Back in the kitchen, Morrison looked out the window to where the icy mist was darkening toward twilight and said he had to be leaving. He was still saying his good-byes when Gib swallowed a lump in his throat and asked, "You going to be taking Ghost with you?" He swallowed again. "Tonight?" Mr. Morrison looked out the window again before he shook his head.

"Don't think I want to start out with him this late in the day," he said. Gib's lump went down some. He was being foolish and he knew it. He'd known all along that Ghost would be claimed as soon as the phone lines were back in. And now, at least he didn't have to see him returned to the same person who had beaten him. But even so, it surely was going to be hard to see him go.

"I'll be back for the horse tomorrow," Morrison was saying, "that is, if that would be all right with Mrs. Thornton." Miss Hooper said she was sure it would be. In the storm porch Morrison told Gib not to bother to go to the barn with him, but Gib said he hadn't groomed the gray yet, so he'd just tag along.

Back in the barn Gib started the currying while Morrison tightened the cinch on the buckskin. But then instead of riding right off, he came over to watch. He went on watching while Ghost nudged Gib's pockets, looking for carrots, and nodded appreciatively when the comb hit an itchy place on his back. But when the buckskin stuck his Roman-nosed head over the stall door Ghost squealed and threatened to bite. A few minutes after that Morrison said,

"How would you like to help out tomorrow, Gibson? Help me get your friend there back to the Circle Bar?"

"Help?" Gib asked. "You mean ride him over there?"

Morrison nodded and then shook his head. "Ride one of yours and lead him, I imagine." His grin looked embarrassed. "I've never had much luck with him, riding or leading, and as he just demonstrated, he and old Bucky here don't get along well at all. If he started something with Bucky while we're out on the road I'm afraid he might get away from me and be on the loose again."

So Gib said he'd be glad to help if Mrs. Thornton didn't mind. Morrison said he didn't think that would be a problem, and then he left. Gib watched him sauntering out of the barn, tugging up his fancy chaps, before he swung up onto the buckskin. Partway across the barnyard he turned in the saddle, lifted his big Stetson, and waved it at Gib. Gib waved back. As he went back to finish the grooming he couldn't help grinning a little as he thought about all the switching around his feelings had done lately concerning the owner of the Circle Bar.

Gib had never exactly hated Morrison the way Livy said she did, but he guessed he'd been influenced some by the things she said about him. And then there had been those few minutes when he'd found out who Ghost belonged to, before he heard about Dettner. For those few minutes he'd hated Morrison worse than poison.

But now . . . Gib shrugged. It was easy to see the man cared a lot about cattle ranching—and about horses too. Gib looked across the corridor at Silky and thought that anybody who got a fire in his belly from looking at Black Silk couldn't be all bad.

Chapter 21

————◆◆◆————

Right at first when Gib asked Missus Julia if he could ride Silky and lead Ghost back to the Circle Bar Ranch, she didn't seem to like the idea very much. But after he'd explained how the gray hated Morrison's buckskin but was pretty friendly with Silky, she decided it would be all right. It was later that night when he and Livy were playing dominoes before he found out it definitely wasn't all right with Livy. He should have known. Everything about Mr. Morrison was all wrong with Livy. For one thing, she wasn't at all sure that it had been a mysterious bronco-buster named Dettner who had beaten Ghost. "How do you know Morrison didn't just make Dettner up so he wouldn't have to take the blame?" she wanted to know.

Gib shook his head. "No, that couldn't be it," he said. "Remember, Hy knew all about Dettner, about how he had a mean streak as wide as the Mississippi?"

Livy leaned forward and shook her finger in Gib's face. "Well, maybe so. But what I think is that anybody who'd steal someone's ranch would probably beat horses too."

Gib played another domino before he said, "You know, you never have explained that to me. At least not so as I got it straight. How did Mr. Morrison manage to do all that land stealing?"

The only answer he got was a squinty-eyed stare and a big sigh. They went on with their game, though, for a while longer. It wasn't until Gib mentioned that he was going to help Morrison get Ghost back to his ranch the next day that Livy really got her back up.

"Tomo . . . ," she started to squeal, and then she glanced over to where her mother and Miss Hooper were playing cards. "Tomorrow?" Her whisper was still pretty fierce. "You can't ride all the way to the Circle Bar tomorrow. We were supposed to have a long riding lesson. It's my last chance to have one before school starts."

After Livy got up and flounced out of the room Missus Julia called Gib over to where she and Miss Hooper were playing cards. Her smile was sympathetic as she asked, "What's the matter now, Gib?"

Gib shook his head. "It's about Mr. Morrison," he said, and before he could say any more both of the ladies raised their eyebrows and nodded. But they didn't say anything else right then. It wasn't until later when Missus Julia had gone to bed that Miss Hooper tried to explain why Livy hated Mr. Morrison.

"It started when Mr. Thornton began urging Julia to sell off most of the acreage," Miss Hooper told Gib.

"Why would he do that?" Gib asked.

"Why indeed? After her father's death Julia had been running the ranch quite well, until the accident. But then, with Julia an invalid, Henry decided they ought to sell. He had no interest in ranching, and he needed the money for an investment his bank was making. Julia didn't agree, but there wasn't much she could do. As it turned out it was quite a spell before Mr. Thornton had any luck finding a buyer. But then along comes Mr. Clark Morrison, fresh from the big city and crazy as a loon about everything concerning cattle ranching and the Wild West."

Miss Hooper's frown was halfway amused as she went on, "Green as grass he was. Everybody said there was no way he was going to make a success out of running a cattle ranch. But he had lots of enthusiasm and a great deal of money."

"But why does Livy hate him so?" Gib asked. "Doesn't sound to me like he really stole anything."

Miss Hooper shrugged. "It's hard to say. Except she felt that the sale of the land was the reason her parents were so unhappy. Seemed like she had to find someone to blame besides her mother and father."

Gib nodded slowly, remembering how Livy had hated him for the same reason because, way back before he was sent to the orphanage, the Thorntons had quarreled over whether to adopt him. Missus Julia had lost then, and it looked like she'd lost again about selling her land. Miss Hooper was still talking while Gib was thinking, but when he started listening again she was saying something about Morrison losing a lot of his start-up herd through mismanagement.

"That's what I was wondering about," Gib said. "It's like Hy says, I guess."

"What's that?" Miss Hooper asked.

"That Mr. Morrison's got more money than sense," Gib told her.

Gib didn't get much sleep that night. It seemed like there were a whole lot of things he had to deal with, and most of them were worrisome. First off there was the fact that he and Livy probably weren't speaking again, which meant that riding to school together was going to be a pretty uncomfortable experience, if not downright embarrassing.

And then there was school itself. Over the holidays, what with all the other things occupying his mind, he'd hardly given a thought to Longford School. Things like Hy's influenza and Livy's riding lessons and, most of all, Ghost himself had shoved punier worries like Rodney and Alvin to the back of his mind. But now here it was the new year and school would be starting the day after tomorrow.

But out in front of the day after tomorrow came tomorrow itself, when he'd be riding Silky and leading Ghost back to the Morrison spread. There were mixed feelings there too. Riding Silky, not in the corral or barnyard but out on the open road, would be fine. Real good to think about, actually. But having to say good-bye to Ghost once they got there was something else again.

To say good-bye to Ghost. Gib shook his head, rolling it back and forth on the pillow, reminding himself again that he'd known from the very beginning that Ghost would have to go sooner or later. But that kind of remembering didn't help much. Not when he thought about how wild and frightened and angry the gray had been when he first showed up, and how, little by little, he'd learned to trust. To trust Gib and maybe even to like him a little.

Lying there in the cold room under a lot of warm quilts and blankets, Gib smiled a little, remembering. "All right," he told himself. "What he liked most probably was the carrots, but he was really beginning to like me too." But that wasn't a thought that helped a great deal, not when he was trying to feel all right about losing Ghost tomorrow.

Just as he'd said he would, Mr. Morrison showed up at the Rocking M early the next day. Gib had just finished the morning chores and was heading for the kitchen with a pail of steaming milk, when Morrison rode into the yard and on over to the hitching rack outside of the barn. He left Bucky at the rack and came on into the house, stomping the snow off his boots in the storm porch but not even stopping to take off his heavy jacket.

Mrs. Thornton and Miss Hooper were still at the table and Mr. Morrison made his usual fuss over them, bowing over their hands and saying flowery things about how they were looking and how good it was to see them again. When Mrs. Perry asked him to have a cup of hot coffee before he started the long ride home he sat down for a minute, warming his hands on the cup and chatting with everyone. Or at least with everyone except Livy. Livy hadn't been speaking to Gib all morning, and when Morrison showed up it didn't take long for her to make it clear she wasn't speaking to him either.

Before they left, Missus Julia told Gib to be careful and to start back in plenty of time to get home before dark. Gib promised he would.

Out in the barn, while Gib was saddling Silky, Mr. Morrison stood around talking, mostly about Ghost. And he called him Ghost too, instead of Famous Fox. When Gib asked, "Ghost?" Morrison shrugged and answered, "I've been thinking about a stable name for him ever since I got him. Famous Fox never did seem like something you could call a cow pony, not even a hot-blooded one." He grinned. "Oh, I thought up a few names for him when he threw me off, but nothing I'd want to repeat around women or children."

They both laughed. "So now, Ghost it is. All right?" Gib said he liked the idea just fine.

When Gib led Silky out to the hitching rack, Morrison was already up on Bucky and halfway across the yard. Hurrying back to the tack room, Gib grabbed a heavy halter and lead rope, and stashed a couple of carrots in his jacket pockets, before he headed for Ghost's stall.

The big gray came to meet him at the stall door, nickering and nudging and looking to find where the carrots were hidden. As soon as he'd chomped them up he accepted the halter without any fuss at all. While he buckled the cheek strap, Gib told Ghost what a good fellow he was, shoving the words out past a tightness that had grabbed his throat when he thought about it being the last time they'd play that find-the-carrot game together.

Morrison was still waiting halfway across the yard when Gib led Ghost out of the barn. He went on watching while Ghost and Silky greeted each other with friendly snorts and Gib mounted and snubbed Ghost's lead rope around his saddle horn.

Ghost and Silky both pranced around some going down the drive but not like they were out to cause any trouble. Just kind of showing off for each other. And once they were out on the main road they both settled down in good order. No trouble at all except once or twice when Morrison got too close, and Ghost squealed and tried to start something with Bucky.

The ride to the Morrison ranch took almost two hours. The snow had frozen into sharp ridges so the footing was pretty tricky. What with watching for ruts and ridges, and having to keep Ghost and Bucky out of biting range, it took some concentration to keep things going smoothly. The pale, sickly-looking sun was straight overhead before they turned off the main road onto the narrow, rutted lane that led to Morrison's Circle Bar Ranch.

The ranch buildings were in a dip in the prairie where, a long way off to the west, you could see some rugged foothills rising up against the sky. The main house was strong and solid-looking, with lots of open veranda space. There were several outbuildings too, all of them well made and sturdy but with that raw-around-the-edges, newly built look. One was a long, low building that appeared to be a bunkhouse, and beyond that there was a huge barn. Next came a stable, and farther out some very large corrals. Everything had that stiff, new look about it. But someday, Gib thought, when time had settled things down a little and the spindly little trees around the house had grown up, it might look almost as good as the Rocking M.

Up ahead Mr. Morrison pulled Bucky to a stop and called, "Well, there it is, Gibson. What do you think of my spread?"

Gib shouted back that it looked just fine. He was trying to think what else to say when Mr. Morrison shouted just what Gib was thinking. "Won't be too bad once the trees get up." He went on shouting then, telling Gib to follow him to the stable, and then they'd go in for a bite to eat.

Morrison galloped on ahead and Gib followed as best he could, but it turned out not to be easy. Ghost, who had been following along nicely out on the open road, suddenly began to fight the lead, prancing and plunging and throwing his head. He fought harder as they passed the barn, almost jerking the smaller mare off her feet. Just beyond the barn Gib pulled up and jumped down. While Silky backed away, holding the lead rope tight, Gib walked along it to the snorting, quivering gray. "Hush, now. Take it easy," he kept saying, and after a minute or two the big horse began to listen. Cocking his ears in Gib's direction, he had begun to quiet when someone yelled, "Stay back, kid. Let me handle this." And then suddenly everything fell apart.

Three men had come out of the bunkhouse and two of them were running toward Gib and Ghost. From the other direction Morrison was running too. And Ghost was going crazy. Snorting, plunging, and rearing, he fought the rope, tugging Gib and Silky after him. One of the men reached Gib and was trying to pull him away when Ghost attacked, squealing and trying to bite. The man retreated quickly and Gib took over again. Then Morrison started yelling, and all three of the strangers began backing off. "Get back. Leave the boy alone," Morrison was yelling. "He knows what he's doing." The three men backed off, and a few minutes later,

Gib led Silky and the still-quivering gray into the stable, with Morrison bringing up the rear.

The stable was a fancy one with brick-paved corridors and wrought-iron decorations over the stall doors. While Morrison took care of Silky, Gib led Ghost on down to a large, roomy stall where the words *Famous Fox* were burnt into a wooden plate.

Ghost was still nervous and spooky. As Gib led him into the stall his eyes were rolling wildly, and his ears were flicking in every direction. Gib kept telling him it was going to be all right. "He's gone, boy," he said, soft and easy. "That miserable horse beater is gone for good. You're going to be just fine here."

Outside the stall door, Gib stopped for a last look at the beautiful dapple gray. He looked long and hard at the well-shaped head, the rounded crest with its heavy mane, the dappled flanks and long, straight legs. Then, fighting against burning eyes and a tightening throat, he said again, this time mainly to himself, "He's going to be just fine here."

When Gib finally turned away he saw that Morrison was there behind him, just outside the stall, along with the three other men. Dressed in denim and leather and wearing riding boots, they looked to be cowhands, employees of the Circle Bar.

"Gibson," Mr. Morrison was saying, "these are some of the Circle Bar hands. Len Barker here, and this is . . ." He went on with the introductions but Gib wasn't listening too well. Still struggling with a tight throat and eyes that threatened to overflow, he could only nod and pretend to smile as each of the cowhands grabbed his hand and said things about his handling of the gray.

"Nice going, kid," one of the men said, and someone else added, "What'd you say to that gray devil? Really settled him down in good order, you did." Gib just went on trying to smile until Mr. Morrison led him away.

Gib had never seen anything like the interior of Mr. Morrison's house. The main room had an enormous stone fireplace and was paneled with thick slabs of shiny wood. The huge, chunky furniture was covered in leather or cowhide, and the chandelier was a wagon wheel, or at least was supposed to look like one. The kitchen was pretty impressive too, long and wide with table space for maybe eighteen or twenty people.

Right at first there didn't seem to be anyone around except for a short roundish man named Rafe and a woman who seemed to be his wife. But then some others began to straggle in. The three cowhands that Gib had already met and then two or three others. Rough-looking men, for the most part, with sun-weathered skin and harsh voices. They all sat in a bunch at the far end of the table and, without saying anything to Morrison or Rafe, proceeded to stuff themselves with potatoes and roast beef and thick chunks of corn bread.

Gib liked Rafe right off. While they were eating he talked a lot about horses, particularly about what a fine-looking mare Silky was and how good it was to have the dapple gray back home again, and in such good shape. "Never thought to see him again," Rafe said. "Not after him disappearing in the middle of that big blizzard." Except for Rafe, nobody talked about the gray at all.

Gib left the Circle Bar feeling worried about Ghost. About how he'd started fretting the moment they reached Morrison's spread, as if he was remembering what had happened to him there. Remembering the whipping, of course, but maybe some other things too. Gib hoped it had only been one person who'd mistreated Ghost, and that he'd be fine once he realized that man was gone for good. It wasn't until he and Silky were alone on the open road that Gib forgot to go on worrying.

Riding Silky out there on the open prairie, everything else just faded away. In places where the sun had melted the ice he let her out a little. Let her stretch her legs and burn up some of that cooped-up, hot-blooded energy. And when the going was slower he talked to her, telling her how fast and strong and purely elegant she was. He went on talking to Silky most of the way home.

Chapter 22

———◆◆◆———

Gib had guessed right about one thing: Livy still wasn't speaking to him. At supper that night Missus Julia and Miss Hooper had a lot of questions about the Circle Bar. Missus Julia, especially, was very curious about what Morrison was doing on the land that had once belonged to her family. And when Gib told them about the grand new ranch house and all the other buildings and corrals they were very impressed. "I guess it's true what people are saying," Missus Julia said. "Morrison has spent a fortune building himself a ranching empire, but . . ." Miss Hooper finished the sentence for her. "But he doesn't know the first thing about managing it."

Gib could tell that Livy was interested too, particularly when he told about Morrison's fancy new stables, but she didn't ask any questions. Even though she and Gib would be heading for Longford School on horseback the very next day, she had no questions about that either.

At breakfast the next morning everyone clse was talking about the ride to school, even Hy, who'd insisted on coming downstairs to see them off. Mrs. Perry wanted them both to eat extra big breakfasts, and Hy had lots of advice about how they ought to handle snowdrifts and icy patches and what to tell Ernie, the stablehand at Appleton's.

Gib wasn't worried about the ride. After all, it was farther to the Circle Bar and he and Silky had handled that just fine. But there were some other things he did wonder about. Like what Rodney and Alvin might be up to these days, not to mention how long it would be before Livy started speaking to him again.

Gib was cinching up Lightning's saddle when Livy came into the barn. Dressed in her new divided skirt and bundled up against the cold, she was carrying a big armload of stuff that included her lunch pail, books, presents for her friends, and the dressy skirt she would change into once she got to school. But her lips were still squeezed shut so Gib kept his shut too.

He finished the saddling without saying anything, but then he looked at Livy's armload again and went back to the tack room for a bigger saddlebag. Livy watched him while he fastened it on behind Lightning's saddle and when he reached for her belongings she handed them over without saying a word. Not a word, at least, until he got to her

174

new pleated skirt. All she said then was, "Don't wrinkle it." Those few words turned out to be a kind of hole in the dike, judging by what happened later.

Everyone came out to see them off, even Missus Julia, whose wheelchair had been pushed out onto the veranda, and Hy in his Indian blanket bathrobe. They all waved and Hy and Miss Hooper called last-minute reminders. Miss Hooper wanted Livy to remember to give their study list to the teacher and Hy hollered at Gib to be sure to remind Ernie to put the horses in the best box stalls at the back of the stables.

The first part of the ride, down the long Rocking M drive, was still pretty heavy going, but Livy had done it before. Except for a few squeals when Lightning skidded a little, she stayed pretty calm. Out on the main road the ruts in the snow were wider and in better shape. At that point it became possible to ride side by side, and that was when the talking began. Only slowly at first, about tricky places on the road and how much longer it would take to get to Longford. But then, little by little, other kinds of comments began to sneak in.

There wasn't much farther to go, only a mile or so, when Livy began standing up in the stirrups, trying to see the top of the school's bell tower. When she noticed Gib laughing she said, "I can't wait to see Alicia and all my other friends. I don't suppose you can understand how much I'm looking forward to seeing them again."

Remembering how much time Livy and her friends spent chattering and giggling together, Gib sobered up and said, "Oh, I think I might be able to understand that."

A minute later Livy started fussing at Lightning, thumping him with her heels and jerking up on the reins, making the old roan toss his head and sidestep a little. "I can't wait to have them see me come riding in on horseback," she told Gib. "Especially Alicia."

"Why's that?" Gib asked. "Why especially Alicia?"

"Because she's had her own pony ever since she was three years old. And she always teased me about being afraid of horses," Livy said. Gib could understand that too, but he didn't say so.

A few minutes later Livy started looking at Gib and Silky. Mostly at Silky. She looked for quite a spell at the elegant, high-stepping Thoroughbred mare, before she said, "I do wish I could be the one riding—"

But Gib cut her off on that one. "No, sir, Olivia Thornton!" he said. "No sirree. I'm not going to be the one to give you the say-so to ride Silky." It must have sounded like he meant it because, after staring at him angry-eyed for a second, Livy smiled sweetly. "I know," she said. "You're right. I can't ride Silky. Not yet, anyway." She sighed and stood up in the stirrups again. "We're almost there," she squealed when they made the last turn onto Schoolhouse Road. "I hope Alicia hasn't gone in yet."

Livy was in luck. Even though Alicia had gone in, some girls who were still on the steps ran in and brought her out. Standing on the top stair with some other special friends of Livy's, she jumped up and down, pointing and waving frantically while Livy made Lightning parade back and forth across the school grounds. Gib kept Silky out on the road, and he went on waiting there quietly until he began to worry about getting to Appleton's and back before school started. "Come on, Livy," he called finally. "I've got to get going."

After a final flourish, Livy got down off Lightning close to the schoolhouse and began to take her things out of the saddlebag. The old roan waited patiently while Livy's friends crowded around, making a fuss over him. Riding over to get him, Gib was thinking that it was a good thing Lightning was trained to ground tie, and that he had enough horse sense to know better than to spook at giggling females.

Livy and her friends were just going in the schoolhouse door when the tall blond one named Matilda looked back, pointed at Silky, and squealed excitedly. As Gib picked up Lightning's reins and headed Silky toward town, he caught a glimpse of Livy as she came out and herded Matilda back inside.

At Appleton's Livery Gib turned the horses over to Ernie and reminded him about the box stalls. Ernie, who didn't always pay attention, particularly when he'd been drinking, nodded vaguely until Gib said, "Hy Carter told me to tell you. You know, those nice dry stalls where you used to keep Mr. Thornton's team." That really seemed to get Ernie's attention and he led Silky and Lightning away, muttering something about Mr. Thornton's stalls.

Gib headed for the school then, hiking as fast as he could on the icy ground. When he ran up the schoolhouse steps and dashed in through the door he almost collided with the tall eighth-grade girl named Betsy who usually rang the bell. He was still begging her pardon when Betsy laughed and waved him on toward Miss Elders's room. "Get going, cowboy," she said. "I'll give you ten seconds." Gib arrived in the classroom out of breath and with muddy boots, but at least he was in his seat before the bell started to ring.

Nothing had changed much over Christmas vacation. Miss Elders had a fancy new blouse and a different hairdo, but her eyes and voice could still make everyone in the room, including Rodney Martin, sit up straight and come to attention. The schoolroom still smelled of chalk dust and wet wool, Livy and her friends were full of secrets, Graham had his nose in a big book, and Rodney Martin was watching everything Gib did. Watching and waiting for a chance to stare threateningly with squinted eyes while he stretched his lips in his angry-dog grin.

It was during the lunchtime recess that Rodney walked

past Gib's desk and whacked him on the back of the head with a big encyclopedia. Gib had been reading at the time and he was still staring after Rodney in shocked surprise when Graham Archer came over and asked Gib if he'd like to play catch.

Still rubbing his head, Gib asked, "Play catch? Right now?" He shook his head gingerly to see if his brains were rattling around before he asked, "Did you see that? Did you see Rodney hit me with that book?"

"Yes," Graham said. "I saw it. That's why I think we ought to play catch, right now. I want to explain something to you."

Out on the icy playground Gib and Graham threw a lopsided baseball back and forth while Graham explained what he called Rodney's war game. "Oh, he doesn't call it that." Graham's smile was mostly in his eyes. "Actually, no one does except me. But it occurred to me that you ought to learn something about the rules."

Gib caught the ball and threw it back. "About whose rules?" he asked.

"Oh, I suppose you'd say they're mostly Rodney's." Graham's smile spread to one corner of his mouth. "Not that he puts them into words. Actually I don't think Rodney has that many words in his vocabulary." Graham dropped the ball and ran after it, slipping and sliding on the ice. When he came back he went on explaining. "The rules are that he has to attack his enemies when they're not looking and— here's the important part—when Miss Elders isn't looking either."

Gib quit throwing and walked up to Graham. "Yeah, but what happens then? Doesn't anyone tell Miss Elders?"

Graham put on a horrified expression. "What? Tell on Rodney? No, of course not. Unheard of. Nobody tells on anyone, and especially not on Rodney. That's one of the most important rules."

On the way back into the building Gib said it all sounded pretty hard on Rodney's enemies. Graham thought a moment before he said, "Yes, it is, I suppose. It would be even harder, except there is another rule, besides the one about not tattling. The other rule isn't Rodney's, and I'm not even sure he's figured it out yet. But what that rule says is that other people can help the enemy. Rodney's enemy, that is."

"How do they do that if they can't tell on him?" Gib asked.

"Different ways," Graham said. "Sometimes it's by warning the person who's about to be attacked. Or by getting Miss Elders to look in the right direction at the right moment." His turned-inward smile flashed and disappeared. "For instance, when I first started going to school here in Longford I was one of Rodney's favorite head-thumping victims." Graham's lips twitched and his deep-set eyes flickered. "But then somebody must have decided it wasn't fair."

"What wasn't fair?" Gib asked.

"Oh, it's hard to say exactly. Maybe they just got tired of watching Rodney sneak up on me. Or else they decided it wasn't fair to let Rodney go on whacking me over the head when . . ." The inward smile flickered again. "When it was pretty clear that my brains were all I had going for me." He took out his watch, stared at it, and put it back in his pocket before he added, "The thing is the other players have to *want* to play on your side."

Right at first Gib wasn't sure what Graham was talking about, but after a while it began to make sense. The "other players" were the rest of the class, and they sure enough did help Rodney's enemies now and then. Like Graham, and little old Bertie too. Like that time the whole class started coughing to get Miss Elders's attention when Rodney was about to steal Bertie's lunch. Gib had just started to wonder if anyone had tried to warn him about the encyclopedia attack, when Miss Elders rapped on her desk and everyone quit socializing, and in Gib's case wondering, and got down to work.

The rest of the day was English and arithmetic, and then came the hike back to the stable to pick up the horses. Gib was almost there when a motorcar went by and there were Rodney and Alvin hanging out of the backseat. As they went by they waved and thumbed their noses but they didn't yell anything, which probably meant that they didn't want to attract the attention of the driver, who was probably Rodney's father.

At Appleton's Livery, Ernie staggered out with Lightning and Silky all saddled up and ready to go and, after he'd checked the cinches, Gib headed back to pick up Livy. The ride back to the Rocking M was okay. The horses were eager to get home and Livy was eager to talk about being back at school. It wasn't until after the evening chores, dinner, and homework in the library that Gib had time to ask himself how the day had really been. How going back to Longford School had been for Gibson Whittaker.

It had been, he decided, both good and bad. The worst part had been the whack on the head and the warning it had given him about Rodney and his plans for the future. And the best part? Well, along with the long rides on Silky, it just might be the fact that the eighth-grade bell ringer had called him cowboy. Not orphan or farm-out, but cowboy.

Chapter 23

The next few weeks were more of the same. More wintry weather, spells of heavy snow, and more riding to Longford School five days a week. One thing that was definitely changing for the better, however, was Hy's health. The next time Dr. Whelan came to see Missus Julia, he pronounced Hy well on the road to recovery. Hy was out of bed now and, except in the very worst weather, out of the house, and even doing the morning milking. Which made getting to school on time a lot easier. But one thing Hy wasn't doing much of was riding Lightning. Hy did take his cow pony out a few times on weekends, but only for a very short ride around the barnyard. "Old ponies like Lightnin' need a couple of days off now and agin'," was the way Hy put it.

But he also said he wasn't complaining. When Gib asked him how he felt about Livy riding Lightning to Longford every day, he just grinned and said, " 'Bout time that old un-educated critter started goin' to school." Later on, Gib heard him tell Missus Julia, "I got to take gettin' back into the saddle slow-like, myself. Give my old bones time to git used to it. So don't you worry none about Miss Livy ridin' Lightnin' to school, Missus Julia. She's mighty welcome. Leastways till the school year's over."

But then, one night after supper, Gib overheard another conversation between the two of them on the subject. He'd fallen asleep on the library sofa and when he woke up he heard Missus Julia saying, "I know, Hy. But Lightning is your horse and it's just not right that he's in Longford every day when you could be using him."

Gib rolled over to let them know he was awake but they didn't seem to take notice. Instead Hy went on talking, a deep rumble that Gib couldn't quite make out, but then it was Missus Julia again. "I agree. Black Silk is still too much horse for her, and besides the mare is pretty much . . ." The rest of it trailed off but Gib thought she might have said that Silky was pretty much his. Gibson Whittaker's. It was a thought that really woke him up, but before he could decide whether that was what he'd actually heard, they went on talking. He couldn't make out all of what was being said, but it seemed to be about Livy. Something about Livy and a good-natured Welsh pony.

Gib didn't say anything to Livy about the pony. For one thing, he wasn't sure if he'd heard it just right, and besides he had no idea what she thought of Welsh ponies. If it turned out that she hated them he didn't want to be the one to tell her she was going to get one. But a few days later, during a streak of almost springlike weather, Mr. Appleton showed up at the Rocking M riding his jug-headed sorrel and leading a pretty little pinto gelding. The pinto was small but not as short-legged as most ponies, with a head and neck that hinted at a touch of Arabian blood. Gib guessed right off that Livy wouldn't be able to resist him, and he was right.

Gib had just gone out to take the two horses, Mr. Appleton's sorrel and the pinto, to the barn, when suddenly Livy was right behind him. Behind him and then running past him saying, "Oh, oh, oh." When she was just a couple of feet from the pinto's nose she stopped and stared for a moment before she said, "He's mine, isn't he? Isn't he, Mr. Appleton?"

Gib didn't know if she was just guessing or if she'd overheard something. He knew how good Livy was at overhearing. Or if it really was, as Livy told him later, that she took one look at the pinto and knew she'd been waiting for him all her life, even way back when she'd thought she hated horses. And she also knew his name was Dandy, after the pinto pony her mother once had.

Livy was kind of bouncing around on the tips of her toes and her face was lit up like a Christmas tree. For a moment Gib was afraid she was going to start waving her arms around and maybe even throw them around the pinto's neck, which might have spooked even a good-natured Welsh pony.

"Livy," Gib said, using the tone of voice he'd have used if he'd been trying to quiet an excited Thoroughbred. Before long she glanced his way, giggled, and stopped bouncing. She reached out then quiet and slow, like he'd taught her, and let the pony sniff her hand before she began to pat his face and neck.

It was the very next day that Livy started riding Dandy to school and Lightning went back to being Hy's and nobody else's. And before long Livy was out there in Dandy's stall every spare minute, before school while Gib was doing the morning chores, and even in the evening when they were supposed to be doing their homework.

Dandy turned out to be a great little horse. He was gentle and biddable, but not a bit lazy. He was good to look at too, with that delicate Arabian head and a splatter of sharp-edged black spots on his mostly white hide. Livy said he was just as beautiful as Black Silk, and he'd be even more beautiful once she got him the expensive black saddle and bridle she'd picked out in the Sears, Roebuck catalog.

The weather stayed pretty predictable through February and March and Gibson Whittaker's life at Longford School was downright predictable too. Some of the people in Miss Elders's fifth and sixth grade still called him orphan or farm-out, and even when they didn't, Gib could tell that was what they were thinking.

Most of the time he'd managed to stay one jump ahead of Rodney and Alvin's ambushes. Every now and then he jumped over a foot that was meant to trip him, and once he'd ducked a baseball that got pitched at his head instead of his bat. But there were a couple of times when he did sit down on a tack that someone had put on his seat. Rodney, it seemed, owned a lot of thumbtacks.

And one rainy day Gib opened his lunch pail right there on his desk and found a very dead rat on top of his sandwiches. So Rodney's war game was still going on, and as far as Gib could tell, not many of what Graham called "the other players" were lining up on Gibson Whittaker's side. Nobody warned him about the tacks, for instance, or smelled a rat in time to keep him from opening that lunch pail right there in front of the whole giggling and snickering class.

His grades were more or less predictable too, good ones in English and history and fair to middling in just about everything else. But if there'd been letter grades for "civilized socializing" his probably wouldn't have been much better than D minus.

Miss Elders talked to him about it once. It was at the end of a school day and Gib was heading for the door when she called him up to her desk. For a minute he thought he was in trouble but it turned out she only wanted to suggest that it might be a good idea if he "made an effort to enlarge his circle of friends." After she'd finished Gib told her he'd try, but what he was thinking was that he'd already tried about every way he knew how. He wanted to tell her that he'd spread his socializing loop every place he could think of, and nobody so much as put a hind foot in it. Except for Bertie and Graham, of course. And now and then Livy. Livy, usually, when he least expected it.

The thing with Livy was that she was one part of Gib's life that never had been predictable and probably never would be. She could be mean as sin one minute and sweet as maple sugar the next. Like one day she hadn't been speaking to Gib for most of the morning, but when Clyde Binghampton called him orphan, Livy told Clyde to shut his big mouth. She also said, "You're a fine one to talk, Clyde Binghampton. You're probably an orphan too, and your folks just aren't telling you."

"What you talking about?" Clyde said. "What call you got to say a thing like that?"

Livy had turned her back on him, but she looked over her shoulder to say, "Because all the rest of the Binghamptons are smart and good-looking. Isn't that the truth, Alicia?" Alicia giggled and said she thought so too.

It wasn't until a Saturday morning early in April, one of the first days that really felt like spring, when Mr. Morrison showed up again at the Rocking M. Gib and Hy were both out in the barn at the time. Gib was shoveling out stalls and Hy was pushing the wheelbarrow out to the manure heap every time it got full, and sitting on a feed bin the rest of the time, telling stories about the olden days.

He was telling one about a ranching family named Higgins who used to do some small-time rustling by branding early calves with their sign, no matter what brand their mamas were packing. "Them Higgins brothers," Hy said, "were countin' on them calves bein' weaned by roundup time, like as not. But most of them little fellers didn't see it that way. So roundup comes along and all the reps from other outfits begin to notice all them half-grown Lazy-H calves trailing around after mamas who belonged to other outfits."

Hy was just telling how the whole Higgins clan made a speedy out-of-state migration just before the sheriff got around to paying them a visit, when Morrison loped into the barnyard. But not on Ghost. On that April day he was still riding his big old buckskin.

Mr. Clark Morrison was duded up pretty good in silver-studded chaps and a brand-new Stetson, but he wasn't looking particularly cheerful as he tied Bucky to the hitching rack and came on into the barn. Gib leaned his shovel against the side of the stall, wiped his hands on his trousers, and came out to say howdy.

Morrison was grinning as he shook hands with Hy and thumped Gib on the shoulder. But the grin faded when Hy asked, "How're things shapin' up out at that fancy spread of yourn?"

"Not too well, I'm afraid," Morrison said. "Seems like I had an awful lot of winter kill during that big storm. And then there were a bunch of early calves who didn't make it through."

And when Gib asked about Ghost, Morrison looked even more down in the mouth. Shaking his head, he said that the gray was still making a real nuisance of himself.

When Hy asked what kind of a nuisance Morrison said, "Oh, throwing his head and rearing. Still bolts too. Gets the bit between his teeth and takes off." He was looking a little bit sheepish as he went on, "And not just when I'm riding him. He gives everybody else as much trouble as he gives me." He looked at Gib for a moment. "You know, Gibson, I think you said that he seemed to be settling down pretty well when you were riding him. Isn't that right?"

When Gib agreed that it was, Morrison went on, "So—I was just wondering if you might . . ." He turned and looked at Hy. "And you too, Hy, if you'd like to. If the both of you could come over and size up that rascal, I'd really appreciate it." And that was how it happened that the very next morning, a sunny Sunday morning in April, Gib met up with the Gray Ghost again.

Chapter 24

Right at first Hy turned down Morrison's invitation to visit the Circle Bar, even though he hadn't been over that part of the range since Mr. Thornton sold it. "I surely would like to ride out and see your spread," he told Morrison. "Gib's been telling me what a fine layout you got there. But I promised the ladies I'd drive them in to church tomorrow." He put his hand on Gib's shoulder. "But Gib here could ride over if he's a mind to."

But the next morning Missus Julia wasn't at breakfast and Miss Hooper said her cough was worse and she wasn't feeling well enough to ride that far. So there'd be Bible reading in the library instead, the way there was in bad weather. And Hy was free to ride to the Circle Bar with Gib after all.

When Gib headed for the barn that Sunday morning it was to saddle both Silky and Lightning, and right after breakfast he and Hy started off. Even now, when mud and slush had replaced ice and snow, the ride seemed like a long one. On the way Gib's mind kept going back to January, when he'd last seen Ghost, and even farther back to when the wild-eyed, bloodied-up dapple gray had shown up in the midst of that awful storm. And now, Gib realized, right now in April, he had no idea what to expect where Ghost was concerned. Halfway talking to himself, he said, "Wouldn't be too surprised if Ghost's gone back to being as bad-acting as he was when he first showed up."

"Bad-acting?" Hy asked. "What kind of bad you talking about, boy?" Gib had almost forgotten that Hy had never been told what Ghost had really been like back then. When he started trying to explain Hy interrupted him. "Why didn't I know about that?" he demanded. "I'd never have give you the say-so to handle a bad actor like that all by yourself." Hy's voice was getting louder and angrier. So angry that Lightning turned his head to look back at his noisy rider, flicking his ears and showing the whites of his eyes.

Gib grinned. "That's why you never heard about it," he said. "Because you'd have been out there in the barn in a minute, no matter how sick you were. Miss Hooper told me I wasn't to tell you anything that would get you upset, so I didn't. Besides, Ghost isn't an outlaw. It was just the beating that . . ."

Gib bit his tongue. He'd done it again. This time Hy pulled Lightning to a stop and right there, halfway to the

Circle Bar, Gib had to tell all about the bloody whip marks that had streaked across Ghost's silvery hide the day he drifted in out of the storm. As he listened Hy kept muttering under his breath and when Gib finished the telling he just sat there steaming like a hot teakettle. At last he said, "Any man who'd take a bullwhip to a poor critter like that . . ." He fumed some more before he went on, "Like I been sayin', that Lou Dettner shoulda been strung up years ago."

They went on riding, but every few minutes Hy went back to scolding Gib for not telling him the truth about what was going on out there in the barn back in December.

"I didn't take any chances," Gib kept telling him. "I figured out how to take care of him without letting him get at me. I took it real slow and easy with him, and in just a few days he began to quiet down."

But Hy went on looking at Gib squinty-eyed for quite a while longer before he began to nod and grin. "Well, guess I can believe that part of it. If anybody could talk some comfort into a poor fear-crazy piece of horseflesh it just might be a little feller I know name of Gibson Whittaker." Then he touched his heels to Lightning's flanks and took off at a sudden run. So sudden it took Gib's speedy Silky a minute or two to catch up.

When they trotted down the driveway onto the Circle Bar, Morrison came out to meet them, his long, sharp-edged face split into a friendly grin. He kept saying how glad he was to see them and how much he appreciated their coming all that way to take a look at his good-for-nothing horse.

Hy didn't say a whole lot as Morrison showed him around, but Gib thought he liked the looks of what he was seeing. At least he did until he caught sight of some of Morrison's hired hands. Two of them were sitting on a corral railing. They hollered howdy as Hy walked past, but his answering howdy didn't seem too enthusiastic. When Gib asked, quiet-like so Morrison wouldn't hear him, Hy only shrugged. "Couple of good-for-nothing drifters," was all he said. "Worked for me once a long time ago. But not for long."

They were inside the stable by then and, as they approached his stall, Ghost came to the door nodding and nickering, friendly-like. Gib was relieved to see that he was looking fat and sassy, and that he'd been groomed until his dappled hide shone like silver-spotted moonlight. As he reached out to rub the gray's nose and pat his neck Gib heard a long, low whistle. It was Hy who'd done it. He whistled and then just stood there for a long spell, shaking his head wonderingly, before he said, "Now that there is one of the best-put-together pieces of horseflesh I ever laid eyes on."

Morrison laughed and said, "I thought the same thing when I first saw him, but if you go by the saying 'pretty is as pretty does . . .'" He didn't finish but his meaning was clear as could be. Right at that moment, though, the gray didn't show signs of being any kind of troublemaker. Instead he went on snorting softly and reaching out to nudge Gib with his satiny nose. But when Gib said he looked pretty settled down to him, Morrison laughed. "Oh, he's friendly enough nowadays, except when he has you up there on his back. That's when you have to look out."

"Have trouble saddling him?" Hy asked.

"Not saddling. But he's still hard to get a bridle on." He turned to Gib. "Did you have that kind of trouble with him?"

Gib nodded. "Right at first he was real head-shy," he said. "But after I started using a hackamore he quit fighting it altogether."

"A hackamore?" Morrison looked shocked and even Hy seemed a bit surprised. "Can't imagine riding a bolter like Ghost with only a hackamore," Morrison said. "How'd you manage to stop him when he decided to run? Were you using a hackamore that day I saw you riding him?" He looked embarrassed when Gib said he was. "Must have been too upset to do much noticing," Morrison said. "And I can't imagine how you managed it. I've been using a curb bit with a long shank and even then he's hard to convince."

Gib was beginning to understand the problem. "I think that's it, Mr. Morrison," he said. "I think Ghost has a real tender mouth. Using a rough bit like that probably hurts him so much he kind of goes crazy. Like as not that's why he starts running."

Morrison didn't seem convinced but Gib could tell that Hy was paying attention. "You rode him with a hackamore?" he asked. When Gib assured him that he had, Hy said, "Well, let's see you do it again, then." He turned to Morrison and asked, "That all right by you?"

"Well, all right, if you say so," Morrison told Hy, but he was still shaking his head as he said it.

Morrison was right about Ghost and saddling. Once he'd finished frisking Gib's pockets looking for carrots, he accepted the saddle and the cinching with no protest at all. The trouble began after that. Morrison had sent his fence-sitting cowhands to look for a hackamore, and after a bit they turned up with a top-notch store-bought one, made of horsehair rope and strips of braided leather. It was one of the fanciest hackamores Gib had ever seen, but Ghost didn't like the look of it one little bit. He was throwing his head and threatening to bite, and outside the stall Morrison and Hy, and even the two cowhands, were telling Gib he'd better back off. But Gib kept on talking and showing Ghost how there wasn't any bit there at all. It took a while before the gray was ready to listen but when his head lowered and his ears began to flick Gib knew he had his attention. And sure enough, it wasn't long before he sniffed the hackamore, snorted, sniffed again, and then, real uncertain-like, let Gib put it on his head.

All four of them, Hy, Morrison, and the two cowhands, followed along as Gib led the gray to the corral. Hy wanted to give him a leg up but Gib grabbed the horn and climbed into the saddle even though Ghost was tossing his head and stepping sideways. Gib let him dance for a minute before he began to sit back, using the reins and his voice to tell Ghost that he was being asked to settle down. After two or three turns around the corral Ghost's ears began to flick back like he was listening, and Gib went on talking. "That's it, boy," Gib kept telling him. "I'm not going to hurt you. I'm just asking you to pay attention."

By the time Gib had taken the big gray around the corral a dozen or so times he was beginning to show the training he'd once had, probably way back when he was a colt in the bluegrass country. When Gib let him out a little he did push some to turn a lope into a run, but he never completely quit listening to what the reins were telling him. Before long he began to slow down extra quick when Gib asked him to, as if he were trying to say how grateful he was to be asked polite-like, instead of being tormented by a cruel bit.

Now and then, as they made the turn in front of the corral gate, Gib caught sight of the four faces peering over the top railing. Right at first, Morrison and his two cowhands looked as nervous as treed wildcats, but after a while they were mostly big-eyed with surprise. But Hy's grin started out as proud as punch and went right on having the same slant to it.

When the workout was over Hy went into the ranch house with Mr. Morrison. Gib stayed in the stable, cooling Ghost down and grooming him, and after that taking a look at a couple of dozen spooky mustangs that he just happened to notice in the corral behind the barn.

Hy stayed in the ranch house talking to Morrison for almost an hour. Later, when he and Gib were on their way back to the Rocking M, he began to tell Gib what they'd been discussing. For one thing, Hy said, Mr. Morrison had been asking his advice about some of the problems he'd had during the winter.

"I told him that when that big snow hit he shoulda sent all his hands out to bring the stock in to where they could be reached by hay wagons, or sleds if the wagons couldn't make it," Hy said. He shook his head ruefully. "Seems like those lazy drifters he's been supporting all winter convinced him it warn't no use. Told him the stock were like as not blown halfway across the state by then, to where they'd never be able to find them. So then that worthless bunch holed up in front of the bunkhouse stove, and let half of Morrison's stock starve to death."

Hy muttered some things under his breath for a while. Then he went on, "I told him what I'd've done. I told him if

I'd been his foreman I'd have had that bunch of yellow-livered good-for-nothin's out there bringin' in cattle before they could count to three. Had 'em bringin' in cattle, or else out on the trail lookin' for a new place to spend the winter."

Gib was so wrapped up in hearing about Morrison's problems that it took him a minute to realize when Hy changed the subject. The new one was about Clark Morrison's wanting to hire Gib Whittaker as a part-time wrangler. "Not full time, of course," Hy was saying. "He knows you have to go on with your schoolin'. Seems like what he's askin' is just for you to sign on to do some horse handling now and then on weekends. Says he'd be willing to pay you regular wrangler wages."

Gib couldn't have been more surprised if somebody had asked him to run for mayor, but he knew right away that he liked the idea a whole lot.

Chapter 25

That night after Gib and Hy came back from the Circle Bar, there was a powwow in the library. At least that was what Hy called it when he asked Miss Hooper to arrange for everyone to be there. Miss Hooper referred to it as a family conference, but Gib liked *powwow* better. He could picture the six of them, Missus Julia and Livy, Miss Hooper, Hy, Mrs. Perry, and Gib himself, sitting around a campfire smoking a peace pipe and making plans for the next big buffalo hunt. When he whispered to Livy about it she thought it was funny too.

Livy was in a specially good mood that night because it was her birthday and she'd gotten all the presents she wanted, including the black-and-silver saddle for Dandy. And she'd liked the present Gib had made for her too, a new saddle rack and bridle hook in the tack room, hung low so she didn't have to climb up on a stool to get her tack down.

After they all sat down around the big library table Livy kept catching Gib's eye and pretending she was puffing on a peace pipe and passing it on to Miss Hooper. Nobody else noticed what Livy was up to, but every time she put the imaginary peace pipe up to her lips, Gib had a hard time keeping his face straight.

The subject of the conference started out to be Hy's visit to the Circle Bar and what he thought of what he'd seen there. First of all, Hy had quite a lot to say about the troubles Morrison had been having and what had caused them. "The trouble with that young feller is jist that . . ."

Gib guessed what was coming and he was right. He mouthed the words to Livy and she giggled. And then Hy went ahead and said it, just the way Gib knew he would. "He's got more money than sense," Hy said, and then he went on to tell about how Clark—Hy was calling Morrison Clark now—didn't know beans about running a cattle ranch. And how he'd added to his problems by hiring a couple of losers for foremen. "First he took on that miserable skunk Dettner, and right now there's this Rafe, who's a right nice feller but who don't know much more about cattle ranching than Clark does. And neither one of them's got the gumption to handle a bunch of ornery saddle bums like the ones they got workin' for them," Hy said. "Looks to me like every no-good drifter who ever got hisself blacklisted by the big outfits got word that there's a rich greenhorn in these parts who'd take them on no questions asked. And that's pretty much what poor old Clark has got hisself stuck with."

But then Hy got to the serious part of the powwow. When he asked Missus Julia if it would be all right if he went to the Circle Bar on weekends to help Clark weed out the deadwood and sign up some real cowpunchers, she only smiled and shrugged and said he might as well. Gib wasn't sure how she really felt about it, though. Missus Julia was coughing again that evening, and Gib wondered if she really didn't care if Hy worked for Morrison on weekends, or if she was just feeling too tired to argue. This time it was only Mrs. Perry who objected out loud.

Shaking her head, she said, "Land sakes, Hy Carter, how do you suppose we're going to get the spring plowing and planting done if you're off gallivanting around the county helping other people?" She looked at Gib. "This boy's a right hard worker but there's no way he can do it all. Specially now that he's going to school."

Hy chuckled. "Now, hold your horses there, Delia. Before you start jumping down my throat wait till you hear the rest of what I have to tell you. What Mr. Morrison is offerin' is that if I help out on his spread, he'll have Rafe come over here to give us a hand with the plowing and suchlike. Rafe's a sodbuster born and bred so you ought to git a lot better farm crop out of him that you'd ever get from a couple of saddle bums like me and Gib here." He grinned at Mrs. Perry and reached over to pat her hand before she could snatch it away. "And Rafe's wife, Liza, says she'd be glad to ride over and help with the canning and jam making when harvesttime comes."

Mrs. Perry was shaking her head sadly when Hy began to explain, but once she'd had time to think over what she was hearing, she cheered up considerably.

Gib and Livy kept fooling around with the powwow idea until Hy started talking about Morrison's offer to hire Gib as a kind of part-time wrangler. "Wants him just on weekends till school is out," Hy told them. "To work with the gray some, and maybe see what he can do with a couple of green-broke mustangs Morrison bought from Appleton a while back." He was grinning as he went on, "Wants to pay real good wages too."

All the ladies, Missus Julia and Miss Hooper and Mrs. Perry too, seemed to think that would be just fine. Miss Hooper said she was very impressed that Mr. Morrison had such faith in Gib's horse-handling ability, but that she wanted to remind Gib that he mustn't let broncobusting interfere with schoolwork. And Missus Julia said she was so proud of Gib's wonderful skill with horses. "And your mother would have been proud too," she added. Gib ducked his head but his warm face cooled off some when he glanced up and saw the way Livy was looking at him.

Sure enough, Livy wasn't speaking to him again. Not for the rest of the evening, or the next day either. Not at breakfast or supper or on the ride into Longford. The not-speaking horseback rides weren't too uncomfortable, Gib discovered. Not nearly as bad as not-speaking buggy rides had been, where you had to sit side by side trying to remember not to say anything or even look in the wrong direction. On horseback all Gib had to do was hold Silky back out of speaking distance, but close enough so that he could catch up if Livy and Dandy ran into any sort of trouble. Then when they got to school he'd catch up long enough for a silent, frowning Livy to get her books out of the saddlebag and hand him Dandy's reins before he headed toward Appleton's Livery Stable.

It wasn't until Thursday evening at the supper table that things with Livy began to change. Hy had been carrying on about Clark's new ranch buildings. About the big ranch house especially, with its "half-acre parlor," and how grand the stable was. "Them horses of his has better living quarters than a whole lot of people do, let me tell you," he was saying, when Livy mumbled, "I'd surely like to have a chance to see a stable like that."

If Hy was surprised he didn't say so. One of his eyebrows did shoot up a little, but he didn't grin, and he certainly didn't mention anything about stolen property. "Well, why don't you come see it, then?" was all he said. "Why don't you come along with Gib and me on Saturday?"

For a second Livy stared at Hy but then she looked at her mother, and when Missus Julia nodded Livy said, "All right, I will," right out loud, and then she went on talking, to her mother at first and then to everybody. Even to Gib.

So the not-speaking problem was over for the time being. Another thing that seemed to be just about over was Livy's suspicions about Clark Morrison. That first Saturday when she rode along with Hy and Gib to the Circle Bar, Mr. Morrison took her around to see the house and stables. And he also made an extra big fuss over Dandy. That seemed to do it.

Livy spent the rest of the day sitting on the fence watching Gib give the gray a long workout, or else tagging along after Hy and Mr. Morrison. On the ride home that afternoon Livy had a lot of interesting things to say about the Circle Bar Ranch. One of the most interesting things, Gib thought, was what she'd stopped saying, all that stuff about it being on stolen land.

That whole month was a busy time for Gib. School during the week, and then weekends at the Circle Bar, with barn work back at home squeezed into spare minutes here and there. Not much time to think about problems at school, or to worry over the useless old question about who Gibson Whittaker was and where he really belonged. But then on one Sunday evening in late April that old question got answered.

Gib had gone up to bed early that night, tired out from

the long ride and the day's work at the Circle Bar. He was just about to turn out the light when suddenly there was the sound of running footsteps in the hall, and then a frantic knocking on his bedroom door.

"Gib, Gib." It was Livy's voice and Gib knew right away that something was terribly wrong.

Pulling on his pants, he tried to shove his nightshirt down inside them, gave up, and opened the door. Livy, a tousled-headed, tear-streaked Livy, burst in, threw herself facedown across his bed, and sobbed hysterically. All kinds of fearful ideas crossed Gib's mind. Somebody—Missus Julia, Miss Hooper, or maybe even Livy herself—was sick. Or maybe even dying.

"Livy? Livy, what is it?" he kept saying. "What's the matter?" Standing there helplessly, he kept wondering whether to go on waiting, or maybe to pull her up off the bed and give her a good shake.

He was leaning toward trying the shaking when, with her face still buried in her arms, she began to talk. "We're going away," she said. "We're leaving the Rocking M and going to live in California. We're leaving our house and the Rocking M, and my school and friends and . . ." The sobs became longer and louder, drowning out the words. ". . . and"—more sobs—"and Dandy too. I can't even take Dandy with me."

Gib didn't believe it. "I don't see how that could be," he said. "They wouldn't do that. Missus Julia wouldn't leave the Rocking M. You must have . . ." He paused, thinking about how good Livy had always been at eavesdropping. "You must have overheard it wrong."

"No. No, I didn't." Livy sat up and, wiping her eyes and cheeks with both hands, she glared at Gib. "I didn't overhear it. They told me to my face. Mama and Miss Hooper did. Dr. Whelan was here again today and he says that Mama has to go to a warmer climate before next winter. And he's already making the arrangements for Mama at a place that he knows about. And Miss Hooper and I have to go too."

Gib stared at Livy. "Does Doc Whelan think Missus Julia is . . ." He paused and swallowed hard. "Is she real sick?" he asked.

Livy broke off crying and stared at Gib. "No. He says she's not real sick. At least not yet. But he thinks she might be, if she had another winter as bad as this one. So they're going to this place where Mama can have some special treatments and Miss Hooper will have to be there to take care of her. And I have to go too." She jumped up then and ran out of the room.

Gib sat on the edge of the bed for a long time thinking about what Livy had said. He didn't believe it. He just couldn't, but he knew he couldn't sleep either, so he got up, put his clothes back on, and went downstairs. No one was in the library or parlor, and at first no one was in the kitchen either. But while he was still standing there wondering if he should go on down the hall to the new wing and knock on a door, Miss Hooper came in, carrying a hot water bottle.

"Well, Gibson," she said. "I thought you went to bed a long time ago." She went to the kitchen range, tested the water in the teapot, and put some more wood on the fire before she turned back and said, "What is it? What . . ." Her frown stiffened. "Olivia hasn't been talking to you, has she?"

Gib nodded miserably. Miss Hooper sighed and pulled out a chair at the kitchen table. "Well," she said. "Well, well. Sit down. Let me try to explain."

Miss Hooper explained very carefully. He could tell that she was trying to make him feel better, and in some ways she did. But one thing that mattered a whole lot wasn't changed at all by what Miss Hooper told him. In fact it only made it worse.

What Miss Hooper had to say was that Dr. Whelan was worried about Missus Julia's health and that it was important for her to get away from the Rocking M and spend some time in a milder climate. Not to stay forever. "Oh, no," she said when Gib asked. "Just for a year or two. Or until her health starts to improve." Miss Hooper reached out and patted Gib on the shoulder. "That's why it's important for you and Hy and Delia to stay right here and take care of the place until the family can come back."

So that was it. No one was dead or dying like he'd

thought at first. He was mighty glad about that. And Miss Hooper hadn't meant to make him feel bad. In fact she probably didn't even know that she had, when she explained about who was going to California and who would be staying behind. Gib was to stay on the Rocking M with Hy and Mrs. Perry, Miss Hooper said. Missus Julia had said that papers couldn't make the difference, and Gib believed that was true. But there was a difference and Miss Hooper had pretty much pointed it out. It would just be the *family* who would be going away.

So, now I know who I am and who I'm not, Gib thought. After Miss Hooper finished explaining he went up to his room and got back into his nightshirt. But he didn't go to sleep for a long time.

Chapter 26

———◆◆◆◆◆———

The next day began with a warm, bright sunrise. A spring morning with the prairie greening and the fruit trees in Mrs. Perry's orchard coming into blossom. But inside the Rocking M ranch house it was anything but bright and sunny.

Everyone was at the table early that morning. Livy's lips were turned down at the corners and her eyes were red and puffy. And the rest of them looked almost as bad. Mrs. Perry's eyes were almost as red as Livy's and Miss Hooper and Missus Julia were silent and solemn. Even Hy's wrinkles seemed deeper and droopier than usual.

There was some talk about going to California, but not much. Missus Julia looked pale and tired and Miss Hooper said that everyone was too upset to discuss it any further for the moment. But there would be, she said, lots of time to talk and make plans before the summer was over, and nothing would be happening until then.

Gib ate his breakfast quickly and hurried out to the barn. To the barn and the horses. It made him feel better, at least a little better, to see them acting just like always, nickering and nodding over their stall doors. He gave Silky and Dandy their oats, and while they were eating he climbed up and threw down hay for the rest of the stock. Then he got on with the saddling. Dandy was ready and waiting at the hitching rack and Gib was just leading Silky out of the barn when Livy came out of the house.

The ride into Longford that morning was a silent affair. Once or twice Gib thought about trying to start a conversation. Like perhaps, "It's not forever. You'll be coming back." But there was a part of him that didn't want to be comforting. A part that kept remembering that nobody had even noticed that he might need some comforting too.

When they were in sight of the school Livy spoke for the first time. Turning to Gib, she said, "Are my eyes still red?"

Gib reined Silky closer to Dandy. "Well," he said, "not very."

The red-rimmed blue eyes squinted angrily. "I hope they are," she said. "I hope everyone asks me what's wrong. Miss Hooper said I wasn't to talk about it yet, but if my friends ask I'll have to tell them. Won't I?" Livy's chin was quivering. "I'll have to tell them, because if I don't they'll just keep on asking."

It was still early when they reached the school and, except for a couple of primary-grade boys throwing a baseball back and forth, there was no one on the playground. As Gib pulled Silky to a stop and reached for Dandy's reins, he said, "Yeah, I suppose you'll have to tell them something."

He had more to say and he said it, but maybe not loud enough for Livy to make out. "You could tell them I'll still be here," was what he muttered. Then, in a tone of voice that left a bitter taste in his mouth, he added, "That ought to cheer them up considerable." Then he spun Silky around and galloped toward Longford. Dandy had to stretch himself some to keep up but, as Gib was finding out, angry feelings were hard to outrun.

The anger was there most of the day. Gib felt it a lot when Livy's friends crowded around her whispering mournfully instead of chattering and giggling as usual—and, as usual, not saying anything at all to Gib. Not even to ask him whether he'd be going away too. Nobody asked Gib about anything. Both Bertie and Graham talked to him some, but all Bertie wanted to talk about was Josephine's split hoof. And Graham, who'd been reading up on the pioneers, wanted to tell Gib about the Donner Party. But at that particular moment Gib found it hard to concentrate on other people's problems. Not even real bad ones like the Donner Party's.

It wasn't until evening that anyone asked Gib how he felt about being asked to stay on at the Rocking M instead of going to California. It was Missus Julia who asked. Right after supper she had Gib push her chair into the library while the others were still in the kitchen.

"I've been wanting to talk to you," she said, while he was still arranging her chair and setting the hand brake. "I can see you're upset about the changes we're all facing. And I certainly understand."

She paused and sighed before she went on, "I'd like to have you come with us, but it's just that so much depends on you here. Hy says he doesn't see how he could manage without you. And then there's Mr. Morrison and the Circle Bar too. I'm sure Mr. Morrison needs your help almost as much as Hy does."

Gib looked away. His face was warming the way it did when he was embarrassed. He continued to look away as Missus Julia went on about how much everyone admired what he could do. Then she said, "Look at me, Gib." And when he did she said, "About school. I want to be sure you understand that nothing, no responsibilities at the Circle Bar or here at home either, will come before your education. I've written to Mr. Shipley, and he will be expecting you to continue at Longford School."

Just about then Livy and Miss Hooper came into the library and Missus Julia patted Gib's hand and said they'd talk some more in a day or two.

Gib's answering grin came easier than he thought it might. And when he said, "That's all right, ma'am. I don't mind staying here," he almost meant it. Now that he'd had time to think about it, he told himself as he got out the dominoes, he didn't really want to live in a city. Didn't want to live in a place where there were people bumping elbows with you and stepping on your heels all the time. Yes, sir, he told himself, he didn't see how he could live in a place like that, no matter who else was going to be there.

He went on telling himself he'd meant what he said until the domino game was over and he had gone up to bed.

Lying there waiting, waiting for a very long time, to go to sleep, he kept reminding himself that he wasn't angry. It wasn't Missus Julia's fault that she had been so poorly all winter. And adoption papers probably wouldn't make any difference, just like she said.

But what still hurt a little was when he recollected how Miss Hooper had put it, about who was going and who wasn't. And the other troublesome part was about staying on at Longford School, where everyone would be sure they knew why he was still there, when the *family* was going away.

Chapter 27

━━━◆◆◆◆◆━━━

It was on the next Friday, just a few days after that conversation with Missus Julia, that Gib and Livy arrived at school a little bit early. Now that the weather was so fine there were ball games before school on nice Fridays, and lots of people came early to play or watch. Usually only the best ballplayers got to play on the Friday morning teams, so Gib, who'd never gotten much practice at game playing at Lovell House, was one of the watchers. Gib, along with all the girls and the primary boys, and even a few parents who sometimes stopped by to watch on their way to do business in Longford.

Livy was still being mournful during the first part of the ride into school that day, but she cheered up some as they got near the playground and the ball game. A crowd was already gathering and, jumping down off Dandy, Livy threw Gib the reins, grabbed her books and lunch, and took off at a run. Gib watched her go for a second before he touched Silky with his heels and set off for the livery stable at a good clip.

When he pulled up in front of Appleton's only a few minutes later it was still pretty early, so he wasn't too surprised when nobody came out to meet him. Gib yelled, "Ernie!" a couple of times before he gave up and led both the horses into the stable. There was still no sign of Ernie as they passed the blacksmith's shop and the tie stalls and went on toward the box stalls at the back of the building.

That was Ernie for you, Gib thought, disappearing on the one morning you needed him to be extra early. But then again, that wasn't really fair to old Ernie. Even though he wasn't too dependable late in the day, when he'd had time to bum a few drinks, he usually was right sober and ready to take care of business in the mornings.

Gib sighed. If he had to take care of the horses and put the tack away himself, he'd surely miss the whole game. He'd just about given up on Ernie entirely, when suddenly there he was sitting on a bale of bedding straw talking to a stranger. A dusty, weather-beaten stranger, wearing a floppy old Stetson that hung down over a long beaky nose. Probably a cowboy drifting through Longford on his way to look for work, Gib thought, and for a moment it crossed his mind to mention that Hy Carter was fixing to hire some extra riders for the Circle Bar's spring roundup. But when he noticed the stranger grab a bottle away from Ernie and stuff it into his own pocket, Gib kept his mouth shut. An early-morning drinker would not be the kind of rider Hy was looking to hire.

About then Ernie noticed Gib and, jumping up, he started to take care of business. His dusty friend stood up too and lent a hand, leading Dandy to his stall while Ernie took care of Silky. "Hey, glad to see you," was all Gib said to Ernie. "Baseball morning. Gotta hurry."

Gib was running by the time he reached the street, but suddenly he slid to a stop. Coming right his way, straight down Main Street, was a high-crested dapple gray carrying a tall man in an extra big Stetson. Sure enough, it was Mr. Morrison, and he was riding Ghost. Riding a calm, sensible-acting Ghost along a busy and noisy downtown street.

Hurrying to the ball game or not, Gib just had to stop for a minute to talk. To talk, and mostly to listen to Mr. Morrison telling him how well Ghost had been doing, and how, even though it was his first trip into town, there'd been no trouble at all.

"I had some business to take care of in town today. Still, I can tell you I thought twice about riding in on this fellow," Mr. Morrison told Gib. "But thanks to you, Gibson, there's been no trouble at all. To you, and to the hackamore, no doubt." Mr. Morrison leaned forward and patted the gray's neck where the hackamore's rein crossed it. "He's been cool as a cucumber, haven't you, old boy?"

217

For a minute or two Gib forgot all about the ball game, rubbing Ghost's nose and neck and telling him how great he was doing, while the big gray nickered and nudged at his pockets. And even turned back to nicker at Gib again as Mr. Morrison led him off toward the stable. Gib couldn't help grinning as he watched Ghost's sensible, head-bobbing walk for just a second longer before he set off running, hoping there was still time to see at least an inning or two before the bell rang.

He'd reached the edge of the school yard, and was trying to get a glimpse of the game over the heads of a lot of other spectators, when a buggy passed on the road and came to a stop near the turnoff to the school's driveway. Gib recognized the driver as a Mr. Wilson who used to work at the Thornton bank, and who drove his two little daughters to school every morning behind the family's sturdy chestnut mare. Gib watched while Mr. Wilson lifted the first little girl down to the ground, turned to get the other one—and froze, staring up the road. He whirled around then and, picking up the first child, he almost threw her back onto the seat. Grabbing for his buggy whip, he ran out into the middle of the road.

By then Gib had heard it too, shouting first, distant voices shouting, and then the rumble of running hooves. The running horse was—Ghost. Still wearing his hacka-more and empty saddle, and every bit as wild-eyed and fear-crazed as he'd been back in December, Ghost passed Gib at a dead run and went on down the road, toward the buggy driver, who was now standing in the middle of the road, waving his whip.

Then Gib was running too, calling out, "No, no. No whip." But Mr. Wilson went on flailing threateningly, trying to stop the runaway, or at least turn him back the way he'd come.

But Ghost didn't stop. Instead he charged at full speed, ears flat, neck extended. He ran straight at Mr. Wilson, who stood his ground until, at the last possible half second, he dropped the whip and flung himself under his buggy. As Ghost shot past he lashed out violently with a hind foot, striking the right wheel with a thud that spooked the mare into a sharp lurch forward. Up in the buggy the little girls were screaming and, from under it, their father was yelling too, as Ghost swerved away into the school grounds—and straight for the ball game.

Ballplayers and spectators, boys and girls of all ages, scattered in every direction as the wild-eyed horse charged across the diamond, heading for the open fields beyond the back fence. But the fence stopped him. Reaching it, he slid to a stop and reared, snorting and pawing the air, before he wheeled and headed straight back the way he'd come.

Gib had reached the middle of the ball field by then and he stopped and stood still, calling out, "Whoa, boy. Whoa there, boy," as Ghost charged directly at him. Head lowered and ears flat, the gray charged until, only a few feet from Gib, he veered into a quick turn and came to a wide-legged, quivering halt.

Standing perfectly still, Gib went on talking, not noticing or caring what he was saying, but aware that Ghost was now certainly listening. He was still pawing the earth and tossing his head, but his ears had started flicking forward. He looked, Gib thought, to be saying how angry and frightened he was, and asking, demanding really, that Gib help him.

At first, when Gib began to move forward, Ghost dodged away, but almost immediately he whirled and stopped again. Still quivering and with white-rimmed eyes, but definitely listening now, he stood his ground when Gib moved again, coming closer. Waiting only long enough to be sure that Ghost knew who he was, he reached out to run his hand along the sweaty gray neck, picked up the reins, and swung up into the saddle.

Ghost lunged forward, not bolting or bucking either but dancing some, tossing his head and floating his long tail. He was quieting, beginning to settle, when someone yelled, "Get down, Gibson! Get down immediately!" It was Mr. Shipley. Running down the school steps and hurrying out across the field, the principal went on yelling. "Get down! And get that horse off the school grounds immediately."

Mr. Shipley meant well, but what he was doing didn't

220

help a bit. Ghost lunged away from him, whirled, reared, and bolted into a dead run. He ran headlong, refusing to listen to the pull of the reins, and was almost to the road before he allowed his plunging run to be turned. Leaning into the turn, Gib tightened it until they were going in a big circle. A crowd-scattering circle that gradually slowed to a gallop, and finally to a high-legged, head-tossing trot. Ghost was moving easy, prancing but under control, when the men who'd chased him all the way from the livery stable appeared on the scene.

There were four or five of them, including Mr. Morrison, who was looking almost as wild-eyed as Ghost himself. The others were Mr. Appleton and Ernie and one or two other volunteer horse catchers. The big-nosed stranger in the floppy Stetson hadn't come along to help out, but right at the moment it didn't occur to Gib to wonder why.

Chapter 28

❧

That morning the scene at Longford School took a long time to straighten itself out. Gib was going to ride Ghost right back to the stable, but it seemed there had to be a good long confab between Mr. Shipley and Mr. Appleton and Mr. Morrison before they'd let him go. Sitting there on Ghost halfway down the school drive, Gib tried, without much success, to hear what was being said. But the three men were keeping their voices down, except now and then when Mr. Shipley came over to chase some students away from the end of the driveway and back onto the playground.

But they kept coming back. Before the confab with Mr. Shipley finished and everything got sorted out, nearly every kid in the school had snuck over to watch Gib and Ghost. Standing around in a good big circle, watching and whispering, they jumped back so quickly they fell over each other if Ghost so much as twitched an ear. But at last the talk was finished and Mr. Morrison came over to tell Gib that he had been excused by the principal to ride Ghost back into town.

Mr. Morrison was grinning as he said that he'd offered to take Ghost back himself. But Mr. Shipley felt that since Gib seemed to have the situation so well in hand, it would be better not to change the equation before "that horse" was safely off school property.

Mr. Morrison laughed, but he sobered up as he said, "I can't imagine what got into him." He rubbed Ghost's nose and the big gray, still sweated up and nervous, stopped tossing his head long enough to nudge back friendly-like. "He was perfectly all right when Ernie led him away," Mr. Morrison said. He looked back to where Ernie was talking to Mr. Wilson, the driver who'd managed to save his neck by diving under his buggy. "What do you suppose old Ernie could have done that spooked him that badly?" he asked.

"No," Gib said uncertainly, "I don't think it was Ernie, but . . ." An idea was beginning to shape itself in Gib's mind. Edging Ghost closer, he whispered, "Mr. Morrison. What does that Lou Dettner feller look like?"

"Why?" Mr. Morrison asked sharply. He stared at Gib for a moment before he even started to answer. He hadn't gotten much farther than the big nose when Gib said, "That's him. That must have been the man I saw in the stable this morning. I'll bet anything Lou Dettner was right there in Appleton's Livery this morning."

Mr. Morrison stared at Gib while his face went dark and slitty-eyed. Then he whirled around and headed toward Ernie who was still standing at the edge of the road. Gib followed along on Ghost.

"Yes, sir, Mr. Morrison," Ernie was saying when Gib got within earshot. "Looked to be a poor cowpoke who just drifted in on a ganted-up mustang. Asked me if he could put the skinny critter out in the corral fer overnight while he bedded down in the loft. But then this morning . . ."

Ernie shook his head wonderingly. "I don't rightly know what happened, Mr. Morrison, 'cept when I led that dapple gray past where that feller was jist standing outside of one of the box stalls, all of a sudden all hell busted loose." He gestured toward Ghost. "Started snorting and squealing, he did, and struck out at that stranger with both front feet like he was trying to stomp him into the ground. Stranger feller grabbed up a piece of two-by-four and started swinging, but that there horse kept comin' at him till he dropped his club and went over the stall door. Went headfirst right over that there door. And when the gray seen he couldn't get at the feller he just took off and started running down Main Street."

Ernie stopped then to catch his breath and to try to answer the question that Morrison had been asking over and over again for some time. "Don't rightly know, sir. Didn't say exactly. Except for Lou. Purty sure he said his callin' name was Lou."

Without asking any more questions Mr. Morrison began to run toward town. Gib let Ghost trot alongside until they were out of sight of the school, when he jumped down and let Morrison take over. As he nudged Ghost into a run Mr. Morrison called back to say he was going to look for the sheriff.

The rest of the day gradually settled back into the ordinary routine. The kind of school day most people might expect on any Friday in May. Most people maybe, but not Gib Whittaker.

Like for instance what happened about Rodney and the thumbtack. It was right after lunch and Miss Elders was writing questions about the Monroe Doctrine on the blackboard. Everyone was busy writing answers when Gib's pencil lead broke. He was heading for the sharpener when there was a loud thumping noise like a lot of people banging on their desks all at once. Gib looked around in time to see the whole class watching Miss Elders, who had turned quickly away from the blackboard to see what was making the noise. She'd turned just in time to see Rodney Martin putting a thumbtack on Gib's chair.

So Rodney got sent to the principal's office. As he walked

out the door, a lot of people looked at Gib and grinned. Gib grinned back, and a little later there was a note from Graham on his desk. The note said, "See? What did I tell you?"

After school was out that afternoon Livy decided she wanted to walk to town with Gib instead of waiting for him to come back with the horses. What she told Miss Elders was that she needed to buy some notebook paper at the Emporium, but as soon as she and Gib started off she told him she didn't really need any paper.

"I just had to talk to you," she told him, skipping along like she had to do to keep up with his long legs. "I just have to know what was wrong with Ghost this morning. Everyone's guessing, but no one knows for sure. And they were all asking me."

When Gib told her about the stranger who was probably Lou Dettner she got so excited her skip turned into a kind of gallop. A few minutes later when they got to Appleton's Livery nobody was there but Ernie, but that afternoon he did seem to be pretty sober. At that moment the only thing Ernie seemed to be really full of was talk.

"That Dettner feller was long gone 'fore we got back here," he said. "Saddled up his poor little mustang and lit out, I guess. But the sheriff said he was goin' to keep an eye out fer him from now on. And I surely will too." Ernie's straggly whiskers quivered fiercely. "Believe me, Miss Thornton, that feller will never get into this place of bisniss agin. Not while yours truly is in charge."

When Ernie finished talking about Dettner he also had a lot to say about what had happened on the school grounds that morning. He went on and on about Gib and what he'd done, and what everyone thought about it. Gib's face got real hot. He finally managed to interrupt long enough to ask if the horses were ready. When Ernie said they were, Gib hurried off to get them while Ernie and Livy and a couple of Livy's friends, who had happened by on their way to the Emporium, went on gabbing about Ghost and Gib.

When Gib came back leading Silky and Dandy, the talk was still going on. He had to remind Livy that her mother would be worrying if they didn't get going soon. Livy finally got up on Dandy and they started off. Her friends waved and called after them, "Good-bye, Livy. Good-bye, cowboy."

Livy was still talking a blue streak when they started for home, but before they got there she'd pretty much run down. However, she looked to have gotten her wind back by the time Gib finished the evening chores. At the supper table the whole family had to hear again about what Gib had done at school that day. Had to hear it for the third or fourth time, actually, because two or three parents of Longford School kids had already phoned Missus Julia about it. And Mr. Morrison had stopped by on his way home from town, too.

Gib was embarrassed, but at the same time he couldn't help liking most of the things that were being said. Things Missus Julia and Miss Hooper said, and particularly what

Hy had to say about what it meant if horses "jist natural took to a feller. Horses know about them things," Hy said, shaking his gnarly old finger in the air. "If them four-legged mind readers takes a real likin' to a feller, like they do to Gib here, you can pretty much count on that feller bein' an all-around square shooter."

For a while that evening, sitting there at the kitchen table listening to Hy and eating Mrs. Perry's famous peach pie, Gib had an unfamiliar feeling. An easy, warm feeling that seemed to be connected to being happy to be where he was right at that minute. *Where* he was and maybe *who* he was too.

For a while he just sat there feeling good, but when he started putting his mind to the reason for it, it all started slipping away. What his mind started saying was that here he finally was, really liking how things were going for him —just as everything was about to change.

It was right about then, as if someone had been reading his mind, that the talk around the table switched over to those very changes. It was Miss Hooper who started it, talking about a trip she was planning to take in June, to look for a good place for her and Missus Julia and Livy to live in California. That was all it took to finish off Gib's good feeling. Right about then his thoughts started into a downward spiral like a bunch of dead leaves falling off a tree. Even the last few bites of peach pie weren't enough to keep him from brooding on how the "family" would be leaving soon and he, Gib, would be left behind at the Rocking M. Gibson Whittaker would be staying on at the Rocking M Ranch, but not because he belonged to the ranching Merrill family, or even to the banking Thornton family, but only because . . .

Belonging, Gib thought. That was what it all amounted to. It was belonging that made you who you were—and who you weren't. His thoughts were still drifting downward when the phone rang and Livy ran to answer it. When she came back a few minutes later she was giggling.

"That was Alicia," she said. "She said she was calling because Paul wants to talk to Gib."

"To me?" Gib couldn't believe it. Paul, Alicia's little brother, was in one of the lower-grade classrooms at Longford School. Gib knew who he was but he'd never talked to him much. Not as far as he could remember. But when he said, "Hello," into the mouthpiece, the high-pitched, wobbly voice that answered did sound a little bit familiar.

"Hello," the little kid's breathy, jittery voice said. "I got some of my friends here, and we just wanted to tell you thank you for saving us from that crazy horse today."

Gib said he didn't think he'd really saved anybody and that the horse wasn't crazy, only scared real bad. While he was talking the little kid kept saying, "Uh-huh, uh-huh," and not much else. But when Gib said, "Well, thanks for calling," the little kid said, "Good-bye, and thank you, cowboy." Then there were some thumping noises and another high-pitched voice said, "Thank you, cowboy." And then another voice said the same thing. And finally one more.

Back in the kitchen Gib had to tell Livy and the rest of them what Paul wanted to talk about. They all laughed, and when Gib told about all the little kids saying, "Good-bye, cowboy," Livy said, "That's what everybody's calling him now." She giggled. "Not Gibson anymore, or . . ." She paused, and Gib figured she was thinking "not orphan, or farm-out" but she didn't say it. "Not anything else," she said. "Just cowboy."

Later, while Gib was having seconds on the peach pie, he decided that maybe he knew who he was after all. And as for belonging . . . Well, there were all kinds of belonging. The kind you were born with and couldn't do anything about. And the kind you worked out for yourself.

He looked around the table and thought about how you would always belong to the people you'd learned to care about. And to yourself too. Belonging to yourself, and to who you were, was pretty important too.

And one more thing he knew about belonging was that he, Gib Whittaker, would always belong with horses.

About the Author

———◆◈◆———

ZILPHA KEATLEY SNYDER has written many distinguished and popular books for young readers, including *The Egypt Game, The Headless Cupid,* and *The Witches of Worm,* all Newbery Honor Books and American Library Association Notable Books for Children. Her most recent books for Delacorte Press are *The Runaways* and *Gib Rides Home,* which *Publishers Weekly,* in a starred review, called "an exceptionally atmospheric and suspenseful tale." Zilpha Keatley Snyder lives in Marin County, California.